THE OAKFORD COURT MYSTERY

By J H Roche

Copyright © 2020 J H ROCHE

All rights reserved

The characters and events portrayed in this book are fictitious. Any similarity to real persons, living or dead, is coincidental and not intended by the author.

No part of this book may be reproduced, or stored in a retrieval system, or transmitted in any form or by any means, electronic, mechanical, photocopying, recording, or otherwise, without express written permission of the publisher.

Cover design by: Dawn Larder

CONTENTS

The OAKFORD COURT MYSTERY	1
Copyright	2
Foreword	5
CHAPTER ONE	7
CHAPTER TWO	18
CHAPTER THREE	25
CHAPTER FOUR	33
CHAPTER FIVE	39
CHAPTER SIX	43
CHAPTER SEVEN	53
CHAPTER EIGHT	61
CHAPTER NINE	66
CHAPTER TEN	72
CHAPTER ELEVEN	82
CHAPTER TWELVE	93
CHAPTER THIRTEEN	98
CHAPTER FOURTEEN	103

CHAPTER FIFTEEN	117
CHAPTER SIXTEEN	123
CHAPTER SEVENTEEN	127
CHAPTER EIGHTEEN	135
CHAPTER NINETEEN	143
CHAPTER TWENTY	151
CHAPTER TWENTY ONE	168
CHAPTER TWENTY TWO	179
CHAPTER TWENTY THREE	187
CHAPTER TWENTY FOUR	204
CHAPTER TWENTY FIVE	210
CHAPTER TWENTY SIX	225
CHAPTER TWENTY SEVEN	253
CHAPTER TWENTY EIGHT	261
CHAPTER TWENTY NINE	279
CHAPTER THIRTY	291
CHAPTER THIRTY ONE	295
CHAPTER THIRTY-TWO	322
EPILOGUE	333
About The Author	339
Enjoyed Reading The Oakford Court Mystery?	341

FOREWORD

A childhood spent reading Agatha Christie books and watching David Suchet, in my opinion at least, the master Hercule Poirot, was the foundation for this novel.

My wonderful Nan, Beryl, had a lifelong fascination with crime and the nature of a 'criminal'. It's something Mrs Christie too seemed to fascinate over and the joy in discovering the simplest and yet most unexpected murderer in her works remains with me today upon a fourth or fifth read.

I am at the very beginning of my career and a world away from the masterpieces of the Queen of Crime, but I hope you enjoy reading this nostalgic homage to her writing as much as I have enjoyed writing it.

Dedicated to Beryl Roche.

CHAPTER ONE

Lord Avery dies

The sound of the phone ringing woke Doctor Carson from a deep sleep.

A trifle irritated to be woken, he reached out and picked up the receiver on the third ring.

'Yes,' he asked in a groggy tone.

'Awfully sorry to disturb you at this hour doctor,' the familiar monotone voice of Harley, the man servant over at Oakford Court, replied down the line.

'Is it Lord Avery? Has the time come?' Doctor Carson had been expecting this call ever since his last house call on the Monday previous.

'I am afraid it would appear so, sir.' Harley replied matter of fact, his voice emotionally calm as any good butler worth his salt should remain. 'Her ladyship has requested that you come at once sir…if it's not too much trouble?'

'Please inform her ladyship that I will be over at once,' Doctor Carson replied in his professional manner.

'Very good sir,' Harley responded before the gentle tap of the receiver ended their call.

Doctor Carson replaced his receiver and sighed. Whilst he knew duty to his parishioners, he wouldn't begrudge someone being kind enough to wait till daylight hours before choosing to meet their maker.

As soon as he had the thought, he banished it shamefully from his head and stood from his bed. Looking back at the empty bed in the night's light, he imagined what life would be like if there was a Mrs Carson. No doubt she would be used to a life of disturbance after some years as a doctor's wife and he mused at the idea of her sleeping peacefully, blissfully unaware of his having to get up and work.

❋ ❋ ❋

It was just 30 minutes later, near 11pm, when Doctor Carson strode up to the foreboding iron gates of the stately home. It was a devilishly cold winter's evening and his shortcut across the moors had done little to ease the chill he now felt. The grand house stood far beyond, an intimidating presence in the darkness with just the entrance light illuminated over the large, enclosed porch showing its grandeur from way back.

As he passed through the creaking gate and made haste down the long driveway, lined either side with giant trees, he couldn't help feeling uneasy in the darkness.

'Pull yourself together man,' he mumbled as he clenched his medical bag and picked up his pace.

The old building's turrets featured ghastly gargoyles, their watchful eyes and imposing shadows only adding to his unease as he got ever closer. With an undeniable sense of relief, he made it to the front door and couldn't fail to notice the bright full moon breaking from a patch of clouds high above. Suddenly, the door opened, and he was met with the ageing butler in his immaculately pressed tails.

'Thank you for attending so promptly doctor,' Harley said with a slight bow of his head, showcasing his receding grey hair.

'Have there been any developments?'

'No sir, his lordship is in and out of sleep.'

'Right, let's not waste anytime then. Please take me to him, Harley.'

'Very good sir, right this way.'

The old butler closed the large oak door behind his guest and preceded into the lobby and on to the large ornate staircase, its cast iron balustrades supporting his ascent as the oak groaned underfoot.

Doctor Carson had taken this very journey countless times over the years but seldom without being awestruck by the grand staircase, large oil paintings of bygone residents and the rather appropriate suit of armour standing guard in the small hallway that split the staircases ascent to the first floor balcony.

The large, squared balcony divided the first-floor bedrooms to each corner, overlooking the ornate parlour below, awash with darkness at this late hour.

Harley knocked gently on the thick door before making his entrance.

'Doctor Carson, your ladyship.'

Lady Avery was a dominant presence in her own right. Sat by her ailing husband's bedside, the lady must be herself in her early 70's but the vividness of her eyes, a sharp emerald glint, and the way she held herself firmly, suggested a much younger woman in spirit.

'Please do come in doctor – I am so grateful for your prompt appearance.'

'Of course, Lady Avery,' he replied, bowing his

head slightly to acknowledge the solemn reason for this unusual late-night visit.

'I am afraid Dickie is frightfully weak,' Lady Avery continued. She was the only member of the family to use her husband's full name 'William' as a rule, the doctor recalled. Most people called him 'Dickie' in the family, although the reason had never been truly clear why, while those locally knew him as 'Lord Avery' or, as Doctor Carson would call him, 'Major'. Her using his affectionate nickname was most irregular – but then, he thought to himself, tonight was a most irregular evening.

As she spoke, his lordship gave the gentlest of squeezes to the hand placed on his and croaked in a weak voice; 'Ellen, let me speak to the doctor for a moment...'

'But of course, darling.'

'Alone,' he replied, in a firmer response that suggested some of the old boy's fire remained from his decorated past as an Army Major.

'I, I will be right outside,' she replied, hesitantly. Her face suggested she was not best pleased to have to vacate the room.

With such obvious reluctance, she took her leave, closing the door behind her. Only once it was fully closed did the old lord speak again.

'Come closer doctor, I fear there isn't much time

left for me now,' he gasped, his blunt and direct tone something the doctor had become accustomed to over the years he had spent as Lord Avery's practitioner.

'Tell me, Major, are you experiencing any sudden changes in temp...'

But before he could finish his sentence, the Major cut him off.

'Dammit man! I'm dying and that's the job lot of it – I don't need your medical qualifications to diagnose this one!' he quipped, almost humorously 'Now, listen up.'

Doctor Carson obeyed and sat quietly in the wooden chair at the bedside.

'That's more like it. Now doctor, I wanted to see you more as a matter of confidence than as a patient.'

'Oh...of course, Major.' Doctor Carson was admittedly intrigued.

'My time is shot doctor, that's the fact of it and as such my good for nothing family will soon be here –vultures the lot of them! But they will come when summoned to get their share. When the time comes - I'd like you to be party to my will being read.'

'Me?!' The doctor exclaimed.

'It's all settled. I had Mckelvie add you as a witness after your last visit,' the Major replied in a matter of fact way. Mr Mckelvie was the long-term family solicitor who the doctor had come across from time to time.

'I don't quite think I understand,' Doctor Carson replied, lost for words at this most unexpected development.

'I like you doctor, always have. A man with good old fashion integrity, that's you! Nothing has rotted you, unlike my lot and you've had more to contend with than most!' Lord Avery begun, his words true enough, as the young doctor had been an only child to a widowed mother, his father dying before he was born, leaving the two of them penniless with little income coming from his mother's job as a household maid.

'My family will get their fair share of the fortune, as is their birthright! But I need you to ensure this old place survives doctor. This estate is my legacy and I suspect some members of this family would sooner sell it and use the profits for a garish modern life in some London apartment,' he growled. The thought was evidently one that had irked him before.

'But Major, how would I possibly....'

Again, his protestations were short-lived.

'I assure you doctor; it is all in hand. Just give me your word and...' The Major himself was cut short, this time by a violent coughing fit that lasted several minutes.

Doctor Carson sat patiently, his head awash with confusion at this extraordinary chain of events. When the Major settled, he spoke once more, weaker this time.

'Well? Can I have you word doctor? You will grant me this dying wish?'

'Certainly Major, as far as I can, I will do what you have asked of me.'

'That a boy! Please doctor, keep this to yourself. When the time comes, you'll know what to do to save this place.'

Doctor Carson could only nod his head in agreement, bewildered by the enigmatic nature of the conversation.

The old boy smiled contently at his wish being granted and shut his eyes. Several moments of silence passed, broken only by the laboured breathing of the dying man.

Then in a moment of silence, the breathing faded entirely. Doctor Carson glanced down at his long-term patient and knew his time was up. He sat a moment longer as the colour began to evaporate from the once proud Lord Avery's sunken face.

He had attended many bedside vigils, many final moments during his career but none were quite as odd as this. The extraordinary last wish of the old man still etched on his mind as he rose and quietly went to the door. Their time together that evening had been brief, just fifteen minutes in total, and yet it had felt like an eternity.

As he opened the large oak door, he half expected the hallway to be empty, but instead found Lady Avery sat on an ornate chaise lounge alongside her only son, Gerald (A couple of years younger than the doctor, he had come from his home in London just the day prior) and her faithful maid Kumba, the long term servant, who had originated from the Caribbean.

Harley was stood just feet away, replacing a used cup and saucer on the tray he had meticulously prepared for Lady Avery during her 'exile' from the room.

At his reappearance, the four of them looked to him, searching for the inevitable confirmation.

'I am terribly sorry,' Doctor Carson began. 'He has passed peacefully'

Those present hung their heads almost in unison. Lady Avery gave a slight, barely audible whimper and pressed a handkerchief to her eyes. Gerald Avery sat silently, hands in his lap and head arched low.

'Thank you, doctor,' he said, calmly.

'I shall make the arrangements first thing in the

morning'

'Yes.... yes, very good,' Gerald replied.

At this point Harley stepped forward and directed an arm gently towards the stairs.

'Perhaps I can show you out doctor?' he stated, his expressionless professional manner untouched.

'Thank you, Harley.' Doctor Carson bowed in Lady Avery's direction; 'Goodbye Lady Avery, I shall be in touch tomorrow.'

'Thank you, doctor.' she replied, as her manner returned to its usual disposition.

With that, Doctor Carson followed Harley back down the stairs and into the eerily cold, silent entrance hall.

'Look after her Ladyship, Harley. I will call the county coroner in the morning once arrangements are made.'

'Yes, sir. I will be at your service, sir,' Harley responded, opening the front door. 'Goodnight doctor.'

'Goodnight.' he replied.

As the door shut and he found himself once more alone in the fresh dim light of the full moon, the doctor found himself thinking once more 'it surely has been the most unusual night....most unusual.'

Something about the expressions on the four faces that greeted the news of Lord Avery's passing had, like many things that night, seemed peculiar to him.

He couldn't quite put his finger on it as he walked down the long driveway but one feeling certainly stuck with him clearly. The look on the faces of her ladyship, her son Gerald and the two servants had not been one of shock or grief....no, on all four faces, it had been one of relief.

'Most unusual,' he murmured as he strolled on.

CHAPTER TWO

Arrangements must be made

Harley was nothing if not a man of habit. His meticulous attention to detail and foresight ensured that even the most uncomfortable of proceedings such as death were handled with all the same efficiency as a dinner party.

Before Lady Avery had even been woken, he had notified the servants of the news, planned for the coroner's arrival, and begun the process of having the guest rooms prepared.

He was in no doubt that the latter of which was a prudent move. The old Lord had been a wealthy man and there was little doubt his dysfunctional family would soon be swarming the court.

From his experience, Harley knew, they seldom visited without an ulterior motive and that motive was nearly always money.

❈ ❈ ❈

At breakfast, Harley's foresight was once again proven invaluable. Lady Avery, dressed as a widow ought, all in black, was preparing plans for her late husband's funeral.

The timing of such a move was not altogether surprising. She was, after all, a practical strong-willed woman.

'No sense moping, Harley,' she quipped as he served her a cup of breakfast tea. 'One must accept death as a matter of course and deal with it.'

'Yes madame – a very healthy approach.'

'Of course, arrangements must be made. I suppose I ought to call Mr Mckelvie and plan for the reading of the will,' she continued, more as a thought to herself than the ever-present butler.

'Very good ma'am,' he dutifully replied as her plate was laid in front of her with its usual arrangement of hard-boiled eggs, a piece of toast and small pots of jam and butter.

'The family will need to be made aware too,' she continued. 'It's a frightful lot of work this. I should hardly think my nerves will cope!'

'I will have the maid bring you some tea in the drawingroom Madame, a source of refreshment is always a good anecdote for tiresome phone calls.'

'That's most helpful, Harley, most helpful,' she began to bite into her lightly buttered toast before another thought came to her.

'I suppose the family will be needed here for a few days whilst we sort the arrangements…Do please get the maids to prepare the guest rooms,' she instructed.

Without delay, the wily old butler replied to the question his years of service had ensured he had already foreseen.

'I have already taken the liberty of instructing the maids to this effect, Madame.'

Lady Avery was hardly surprised by the butler's efficiency. She had grown to be extremely dependent on it over the years.

'Splendid work, Harley – I shall at once begin my calls and then perhaps a walk in the grounds would be good for one's health.'

'I will have your walking boots and coat ready m'lady.' Harley bowed his head as he took his leave from the breakfast parlour to attend to his duties.

Lady Avery finished her breakfast quietly. Death was an awfully tiring business and yet one no doubt inevitable with the passage of time, she mused. Still, having servants as efficient as Harley certainly made it an altogether easier trial!

* * *

The ornate drawing room was set off the side of the main hallway. Its white wooden panelling, ivory colour wallpaper and large bay windows overlooking the grounds made it a most agreeable room. Two large fireplaces with great marble surrounds and two large chandeliers high above, never failed to impress even the most cultured of visitors.

Sat in her favoured window box seat, Lady Avery picked up the telephone receiver from the small side table next to her and made her first call to the firm of 'Reeds, Mckelvie and Reeds,' the Avery family solicitors for over half a century. The two 'Reeds' had since perished but Mr James Mckelvie was a stickler for tradition and so the name had remained unaltered ever since.

Lady Avery's call was answered by the firm's secretary on the second ring.

'Good morning, Reeds, Mckelvie and Reeds,' the youthful voice of the young receptionist declared cheerfully.

'This is Lady Avery – please kindly put me on with Mr Mckelvie at once.'

The dominant voice of the matriarchal Lady made the young aide gulp with nerves.'

'Right…. right away, Lady Avery,' she stuttered in reply.

The incompetence of youth never ceased to amaze Lady Avery. Working at a young age, she felt was simply beyond the capabilities of the average person these days.

'Lady Avery.' Came the voice of an elder gentleman, more versed to dealing with significant customers. 'I am so terribly sorry to hear the news of his lordship's passing.'

How he knew this news didn't surprise or concern Lady Avery. Small rural communities had a way of knowing just about everything before it had even happened, in her experience, and for that news to then get as far afield as London was only a matter of course.

'Thank you, Mr Mckelvie,' she replied as a matter of courtesy. 'I am calling to arrange the reading of my late husband's will at your earliest convenience. I trust you can appreciate the importance of such formalities taking place without delay.'

He could. Especially, he thought, when dealing with a headstrong old woman like Lady Avery.

'Yes of course, Lady Avery – a most prudent approach,' he concurred in his experienced manner. 'However, your late husband's will does specify that all beneficiaries must be present for the reading,' he contributed cautiously, unsure of how much the Lady knew of her husband's strict stipulations.

'Yes, I suspected as much,' was her rather blunt response, devoid of emotion.

'We can help make the necessary arrangements for you, Lady Avery – calling the family members and organising their attendance?'

'That would be most helpful, Mr Mckelvie,' the old lady's tone warming noticeably at the suggestion.

'Of course, Lady Avery, of course. I shall have my man Jenkins make the calls at once,' he replied, keen to placate her ladyship. 'Can we assume that Oakford Court will be readily available to accommodate?'

'Naturally,' she replied.

'Excellent! Well leave it with us Lady Avery and if at all possible, we can read the will this coming Saturday.'

'Thank you, Mr Mckelvie, I sincerely hope we can! Good day to you.'

'Good day, Lady Avery,' he replied, replacing the receiver.

What an extraordinary old woman she is he

thought as he sat quietly at his desk. Pure steel, a trait lost on today's youth.

'Jenkins,' he yelled loudly through the partially open office door.

'Yes, sir?' the aide's head peaked round the door nervously.

'Get me Doctor Carson on the phone.'

'Right away, sir.'

This would be a rather unusual weekend he felt, but then nothing about Lord Avery and Oakford Court had ever struck him as ordinary.

CHAPTER THREE

Richard Haymer returns

He heard the approaching roar of the motor car before he saw it. A growling engine which echoed through the tree-lined avenue of the main drive.

The fascination with these modern engines had never been clear to Harley. 'Give me a horse-drawn carriage or the steam train any day,' he thought to himself as he made his way to the front entrance to perform his duty.

As he did, he saw the Riley Brookland in gun metal green coming spewing up the driveway, a cloud of dust from the gravel below in its midst, coming to an abrupt stop at an awkward angle on the circular loop of the drive.

The young driver removed his goggles and sprung from his seat, sprightly landing on the gravel, a look of satisfaction etched on his face.

'I'll have this beauty up to 70 yet,' he stated proudly.

'Good morning, sir,' Harley acknowledged the cocksure young man.

'Harley, you old dog! I doubt you've changed an inch since I last saw you!' Richard Haymer exclaimed. He hadn't been back to his late uncle's estate in nearly five years and yet first glance told him the old manor has been frozen in time, butler, and all, ever since.

'Thank you, sir. May I take your luggage?'

'No, don't trouble yourself my good man, I travel light!' he replied in his charming way, grabbing his compact leather case from the back of the Riley.

Richard Haymer was a man for the times in every sense – tall, dark and handsome. His good looks, easy charm and wavy brown hair made him popular with the fairer sex, whilst his ability to provide insightful conversation on most subjects made him a worthy adversary in most social standings. As accomplished young men went, Richard Haymer was a well-travelled, much-liked man.

Harley showed his young guest to his room on the first floor and dutifully returned to his chores.

'I wonder if that old dog will ever change? He is as much a part of this stuffy old estate as those god-awful gargoyles,' Haymer thought to himself. The imposing statues had often been a source of nightmares upon his childhood visits to Oakford Court.

Unpacking his case, Richard Haymer took a moment to navigate the wood panelled room with its small fireplace and odd shaped windows looking out at the lakeside grounds in the distance beyond. He had never much cared for the old place and hoped to be back in the somewhat more colourful haunts of the continent before too long. As he opened his bedroom door, he clasped eyes on another familiar sight from the past – Kumba, the family's long-time housekeeper, who Lord Avery had bought back with him from his time in the Caribbean, though Haymer couldn't recall where or when.

'Mr Richard – is that you?!' the old maid said, her exotic accent never ceased to amaze.

'Why Kumba you get more beautiful every time I see you!' he exclaimed affectionately, kissing the maid on both cheeks.

The old maid, dressed as ever in her black and white uniform gushed over the young man's charm: 'Ohh, Mr Richard! You are too kind!' she beamed, her infectious laugh ringing around the hallway.

'Always a pleasure to see you Kumba. I just wish it was under better circumstances,' he replied, a more serious tone as he continued; 'Poor old Uncle Dickie! Suppose he had a good innings – how's Aunt Ellen fairing up?'

'Lady Avery is a…. strong woman,' Kumba replied, picking her words thoughtfully.

'Yes, indeed!' Haymer agreed. 'Well, I suppose I ought to familiarise myself with the old place again, not that much changes!'

'Change is nothing more than a necessity of the seasons, Mr Richard! Oakford lives on, I'm sure about that,' the wily old maid replied in her unique accent, a brilliant smile on her face.

'I have no doubts that you're right!' Haymer replied and smiled sweetly at the maid, though his thoughts said he had very many doubts.

✳ ✳ ✳

As he made his way down to the wood panelled library, nestled in the belly of the house, Haymer stopped to appreciate the eclectic tastes of his late uncle. The ground floor entranceway leading to the library was full to the rafters of 'souvenirs' Lord Avery had picked up on his tours and travels.

Hunting trophies and artwork covered the walls, whilst ornate sculptures and weapons filled the room's vast spaces alongside the more traditional grandfather clock, chiming in concise patterns as it had for generations.

The library was an octagon shape with large bookshelves lining all walls and a fireplace with a grand painting of Lord Avery's father hanging above it. Two large, tall windows allowed the afternoon light to seep through, creeping in stripes up the walls either side of the adjacent fireplace.

The drinks trolley stood as it always had, under the bay of one of the windows. Haymer helped himself to a whisky and lit a cigarette. The books on the shelves had been organised into clear categories with military history, travel and class literature the dominant themes.

Just then the door opened and, in its entrance, stood Gerald Avery, the only son of Lord and Lady Avery. He was just a year younger than Haymer and yet his receding hairline and shorter height meant he was often perceived as the elder, of the two.

'Gerry! How good to see you my chap! So sorry we must be here under such circumstances'

'You never seem to change a blot Haymer, last I heard you were out in the tropics with some tribe of Neanderthals?!' The younger man replied, a much more serious tone to his voice than that of his jovial cousin.

They shook hands, Gerald eyeing Haymer with intense eyes as if trying to read his thoughts.

'I was in Africa for some time yes, fascinating place really – very primitive,' Haymer replied. 'Can I get you a drink, Gerry?'

'Yes…a brandy please'

'Coming right up. So, tell me, Gerry, what have you been up to? I've hardly heard a bean about you in the last couple of years!' He began pouring the brandy from the crystal decanter.

This certainly didn't come as a surprise to Gerald. He doubted very much he had been a favoured topic of discussion when his father communicated with his beloved nephew. He had long felt his parent's affections for their charismatic nephew surpassed their feelings for him and in the case of his father it was a well-known observation.

'I wouldn't expect you had – but I've been working down in London for a very established accountancy firm, 'Sickert and Walters.' Perhaps you've heard of them?'

'Can't say that I have old chap, not much need for

an accountant in my line of work,' he quipped 'but cheers to good honest work!' he raised his glass before knocking back its remnants.

'Quite so, and what exactly is your line of work?' Gerald smugly asked, pretty certain his cousin hadn't held down a job or in fact done a day's work in his life.

'Ah, I'm a bit of a jack-of-all-trades, currently between things at the moment,' Haymer replied vaguely.

'Yes, I imagine you are.' Gerald firmly felt he had gained the upper hand in the conversation as the room fell silent.

The door opened and Lady Avery stepped into the library, dressed once more in her black mourning dress.

'Mother, you need rest – can I fix you a drink?' Gerald stood to attention at the sight of his mother's entrance.

'Oh, stop fussing, Gerald,' she snapped before her tone instantly became more amiable at the sight of her nephew. 'Richard, my dear! I didn't know you had arrived?!'

'Aunt Ellen, darling, it's been too long,' he affectionately took his aunt's hand and kissed it softly.

'It's so good of you to come, Richard – I do hope you will stay a while once this awful business is over?'

'As luck would have it mother, Richard is between jobs,' Gerald chimed in, mischievously.

'Well then, you simply must stay with us. I won't take no for an answer and I want to hear all about your travels.'

'Erm, well yes why not! I would be delighted.' Haymer responded, although Gerald took great satisfaction in suspecting he was anything but.

'Splendid! Oh, you do look awfully like your late father…he'd have been so proud of you,' she beamed at her nephew.

'You're too kind Aunt Ellen. Do join me for a drink won't you dear?'

'A small brandy wouldn't hurt, thank you Richard.'

Gerald couldn't help but roll his eyes. He very much believed that even if Richard had suggested a dip in the lake during the impending snow blizzard, his mother would say anything other than 'splendid idea'.

CHAPTER FOUR

The family reunion

The remaining family members arrived throughout the afternoon, with Lord Avery's only surviving brother the next to turn up. Phillip 'Colonel' Avery was very much a spitting image of his older brother. If not for his more formidable girth and extravagant moustache, one might have struggled to tell the two apart in their years together.

The 'Colonel', as he had always been known, had been a military man like his late brother, although no one actually knew if his rank had been earned or gifted affectionately over the years. A lifelong bachelor, the Colonel was prone to latch on to anyone he could and narrate, at great length, memoirs of his time over in the colonies.

An hour or so after the Colonel arrived, his

youngest sibling, Mrs Celia Langtry followed suit. As the youngest child and only girl in a family of boys, she had married early to an eccentric artist 10 years her senior from Cornwall, much to her family's horror. The pair had eloped and she moved down to the small seaside town of Fowey with the artist, Jeffery Langtry, and his young daughter whose mother had tragically died in childbirth just five years previous.

Tragedy struck again just three years later when Jeffery Langtry's fishing boat capsized at sea during a storm, his body never found. The newly married Mrs Langtry found herself a widow, with a pittance of a legacy and an 8-year-old orphaned child to adopt.

Whilst her brother Lord Avery had never agreed with her decision to elope - and with an artist of all people - he took pity on his young sister and gave her an annual income that, alongside the sale of some of her late husband's work, meant she could maintain the cottage in Fowey with a small staff.

A proud woman, Mrs Langtry had always maintained her family legacy, but she remained devoted to her late husband's memory, a move which ensured she remained somewhat of a black sheep in her own family.

❋ ❋ ❋

The entire family convened for the first time that evening in the dining room. The long table, dim lighting and sombre atmosphere left the conversation wanting to begin with.

Richard Haymer, never a man to let British sensibility get in the way, tried his best to illicit conversation from his dining partners.

'So, what does one do down on the Cornish coast?'

The intended recipient of his question was Miss Lillie Morris, the adopted daughter of Mrs Langtry. In what would be known as an 'English Rose', Miss Morris' fair and pale complexion, blue eyes and light mousey brown hair made her an attractive young woman whose dainty structure suggested a more childlike age than her twenty two years.

'Oh, it is wonderful really – the beaches, the walks, such fresh air! And kind people, the type one would hardly expect to get up in the great smog of the city'

'But surely it's a dull old place when the Great British weather plays its hand?'

'It's not unlike anywhere else in the country where the weather is concerned,' she said, before continuing: 'I suppose bad weather feels awfully foreign to you, Mr Haymer?'

'Call me Richard please! I confess, I've had a

good run of sunshine out in Africa but there's something about 'proper' seasonal weather that really cannot beat home.'

'Jeffrey was always fascinated by the weather, it mattered not whether glorious sunshine or horrendous downpours of rain!' Mrs Langtry reminisced from across the table. 'He couldn't resist the seasons, always saying how vital they were to his work.'

'I'm sure, dear Aunt Cecilia, that his paintings were all the better for such inspiration,' Haymer responded warmly.

'You really must see some of his work Richard!'

'I'd like that very much, I'm sure.'

'Of course, you won't be able to here – pity, the old place could do with an injection of life,' she continued drolly, before realising the insensitive choice of her words. 'Oh Ellen, I do hope you can forgive my careless comment.'

'Nothing to forgive, my dear,' the matriarch replied to her sister-in-law, before taking the opportunity to get her own jibe in.

'Dickie never was a fan of modern art, always said it devalued a room and I'm inclined to agree.'

The tension at the table was palpable as the other guests awaited Mrs Langtry's retort. But it was, in fact, the Colonel who broke the deadlock with his own comment, himself oblivious to the battle brewing around him.

'The Indians used mud more often than not for painting and building houses – extraordinary sight!'

'I doubt that Indians have the right sort of temperament for art,' Gerald chimed up.

'Oh rot! They have quite incredible creativity! The colours they create using chalk really are stunning,' Haymer responded 'The Africans too!'

'You're awfully well-travelled aren't, you Mr Haymer,' Lillie marvelled.

'It's Richard, please' he reiterated, oozing charm.

'A man must travel, dear girl. It broadens the mind in a way not even romance can,' Colonel Avery stated.

The subject of travel took up much of the rest of the conversation, extinguishing any lasting feelings of hostility between Lady Avery and her sister-in-law.

After dinner, Harley came in and spoke discreetly to Lady Avery at the head of the table. She nodded a silent understanding before announcing to the gathered ensemble: 'I have asked Mr Mckelvie and Dr Carson to join us for dinner tomorrow. During the course of the evening, we will have Lord Avery's last will and testament read according to his wishes,' she said in her matter-of-fact way. 'They have graciously agreed'

'No sense prolonging it mother,' Gerald stated, satisfied with the efficiency of his mother's actions.

A sentiment much of the table seemed to agree to. It seemed no one was keen to extend this dysfunctional family reunion any longer than entirely necessary.

CHAPTER FIVE

Snow is to be expected

The next morning saw the first heavy frost of what was predicted to be a harsh winter. Snow was expected to follow suit and with great measure. The dysfunctional household was spread across the estate that morning - the Colonel had opted for a brisk walk through the grounds, Mrs Langtry had remained in her room, a bit under the weather, and her adopted daughter Lillie Morris had decided to join Gerald for a game of chess in the library.

Lady Avery ate breakfast in the breakfast parlour with her favourite nephew Richard Haymer.

'Oh Richard, I can't tell you how glad I am to see you again dear, it has been so long,' Lady Avery cooed over her nephew as he ate his breakfast of kippers and toast.

'Thank you, Aunt Ellen. I just wish I'd made it back here to see old Uncle Dickie…before…' his voice trailed off, regret in his eyes.

'I know, dear, and I know he would have loved to have seen you again after all these years. He never stopped talking about you and really enjoyed hearing all about your adventures in your letters.'

'He was a great man and he'll be sorely missed, that's a fact!'

'Oh, we had begun to worry about you Richard! When you stopped writing, I must confess there was a time when we feared the worst!' Lady Avery continued, recalling the three-month period two years prior when their correspondence with their nephew abruptly stopped during his time in the Congo.

The young man chewed on his breakfast for a moment, before replying.

'I bet you must have my dear! I honestly cannot understand why my letters were not getting through to you! Naturally, I, too, was concerned when I stopped receiving your letters and investigated! That's the trouble with these backwards countries, no accountability or pride in their work! Not like the good old Royal Mail!'

'I know dear, you have explained it all already!

I am just glad you were safe. Poor Dickie lost many a night's sleep with worry.'

Richard Haymer took a long sip of his coffee. He certainly didn't want to continue on this line of conversation, his guilt over that period of time remained sore to this day and now, face-to-face with his frail aunt, he was all too aware of the emotional turmoil they must have faced.

'Well, the important thing, my dear Aunt, is I am here with you now and I assure you I will do all I can to support you during this ghastly time!' he smiled warmly.

She squeezed his extended hand and returned his warm smile. Lady Avery was seldom a sentimental person, but her nephew had always managed to hold a special place in her heart, and she was pleased to have his presence, now more than ever. Yet, something felt different to her, as if his time on the continent had changed him. It was a feeling she shook off as nonsense. Naturally travel could change a man! She had seen the effects first-hand on her late husband and his rather eccentric brother, the Colonel, who she could now see walking down the frozen grounds beyond them.

Perhaps, in a tragedy such as this, there could be positives, she pondered, and, for Lady Avery, the thought of having Richard Haymer back home was indeed particularly positive. Something she hoped could become permanent. Life has a funny way of connecting events like this, she mused, as she watched her nephew enjoy his breakfast.

Lady Avery had no idea just how prophetic her words would become.

CHAPTER SIX

A coincidence on the train

Mr Mckelvie had travelled up to Oakford from London on the 8.56am from Waterloo. For much of the journey he had managed to avoid idle conversation with the old lady and foreign gentleman who shared his berth.

Having firmly read his copy of The Times from cover to cover, he occupied himself with reviewing his notes from his previous meetings with the late Lord Avery and by admiring the Great British countryside out of the carriage window. Such charming, peaceful environments he thought as he caught glimpses of small towns and villages as they passed. A lifelong city dweller, he had rarely made enough time for the country and yet he suspected he really ought to

– an all-round much more civilised setting.

The headline on the front page of The Times read 'Murderer Apprehended'. After a two-day search across London, a man responsible for the grisly death of his wife had, it seemed, finally been caught.

Murder, Mckelvie thought to himself, was certainly a curse of the city. Perhaps, he may just retire out into the country and live a peaceful existence someday. He very much doubted there would be any murder in the countryside – it's much too tranquil, he mused.

At the next station stop, just outside of Exeter, the old lady had disembarked the train, leaving just the foreign gentleman with Mckelvie; a heavyset man in a three-piece suit with jet black hair, a thin moustache neatly spread over his top lip and dark beady eyes behind a pair of reading glasses, sat effortlessly at the end of his nose. He had, moments earlier, asked if he may glance over Mckelvie's newspaper and had since busied himself reading the contents.

He grunted as he put down the paper, removed his spectacles and spoke in the direction of his fellow passenger.

'The human psyche…it's a most marvellous invention but murder it is most foul, most foul!' his heavily accented English apparent as he shook his head.

'A ghastly case that one,' Mckelvie agreed, reluctantly entering the conversation.

'Ghastly indeed, signor...'

'Mckelvie,' the other offered, extending his hand.

'Signor Mckelvie,' the foreigner bowed his head 'my name is Giuseppe Pezzola. Are you travelling on business signor?'

Mckelvie realised his peaceful journey had come to an end prematurely but replied in a kind voice: 'I suppose I am, yes. A client of mine passed away last week.'

'Ah, *le mie condoglianze*! How you say in English? My condolences, signor.' The Italian frowned as he searched for the correct translation from his native tongue.

'Thank you, Mr Pezz...Pezzola,' it was a tricky name to say, Mckelvie thought, hardly rolling off the tongue of a staunch Englishman such as himself. 'Are you travelling on business?'

'I am, signor. I often travel all across Europe for my work,' he replied with an elaborate hand.

'Across Europe? How fascinating. What line of work requires such extensive travel?' Mckelvie enquired, genuinely intrigued for the first time since engaging in conversation with his unusual travel companion.

'Oh, I am in the textiles business,' Pezzola replied, although he appeared to shift uneasily in his chair.

'And that brings you all the way over here?!' Mckelvie marvelled.

'Si, signor, my company, we work with large hotels and country estates providing the best furnishing in some of the finest properties in London, Rome, Milan and Paris.'

'And now you're heading down to the West Country - quite a change of scenery,' Mckelvie chuckled at the thought.

Pezzola laughed heartily, his friendly demeanour returning as his large stomach pressed against his tight shirt.

'It is indeed a rather different spot, but I have business to attend down here, nonetheless. It will be my first time in the, how you say, West Country of Devon.'

Mckelvie chuckled again, the accent of the man really was so peculiar!

'I, myself, hardly ever get the chance to come down to this neck of the woods but it certainly is a beautiful spot – whereabouts are you getting off?'

Pezolla pulled a handwritten piece of paper from his suit pocket and looked at it with a puzzled face. He passed it over and exclaimed: 'I am afraid I cannot say this name!'

Mckelvie obliged, glancing down at the note. He acknowledged: 'Why it's Oakford! That's where I am heading!'

'*Oak...food*?' the Italian said, mimicking his companion as best he could.

'That will do,' Mckelvie said warmly, 'say, whereabouts are you staying?'

'I stay at a place called '*Ind's Head.*'

'Ah, the Hind's Head! Yes, I suspected you might be – hardly anywhere else for us travellers to stay in a village like Oakford.'

'You stay there also?' Pezzola said, surprise on his face.

'I certainly will be, just for a couple of days whilst I attend to my client's wishes.'

'Ah, it is fate then that we are to meet on this train, eh!'

Mckelvie laughed once more. He was beginning to warm to the funny little man, 'It appears it is, yes.'

'Me, signor, I stay just one night before continuing my journey into Cornwall. I confess, this weather it is not so ideal and a night by the fire awaits me I suspect!'

'The winters' certainly get tough down this neck

of the woods and this year is likely to be one of the biggest snowfalls in recent history, least that's what the papers say,' Mckelvie replied.

'How you say *nick of the woods*? What is this?' Pezzola looked confused once more.

Mckelvie chuckled: 'It means this part of the country! Mr Pezzola, you really must learn the local expressions if you are to spend any length of time in the country, especially with a strong dialect such as the Cornish one.'

'Grazie, signor, I think it is good I only have one week in this *nick of the woods*!' he laughed, his large frame moving like a jelly as he did.

'A week eh? Where will you be heading off to after that?'

'I am not so sure, perhaps I go home to Italia or perhaps I continue my work in Eastern Europe. The world, as they say, is my oyster.'

'It really must be quite wonderful to get to travel so much,' Mckelvie mused.

'Travel, it broadens the mind,' Pezzola stated proudly, tapping his head for emphasis.

'Yes, I rather suppose it does! Not one to travel too far myself, call me old fashioned but an Englishman's castle is his home and all that!'

'Ah, si signore, I understand completely. I confess, I love the *Engleesh* but the weather it is not as agreeable! When I feel the cold rain, Italia she tempts me back home to the Mediterranean sunshine!'

Mckelvie nodded his understanding. He had never been to Italy but could well imagine the rolling sun-baked hills of Tuscany held much appeal. Despite his staunch loyalty to his home nation, even a stubborn old Brit like him often longed for a warmer climate, especially during the bitterly cold winters such as this.

The train continued its long, laboured journey as the passing countryside became increasingly blurred by the worsening rain.

'I fear this weather will get worse yet,' Mckelvie said aloud, looking out of the window at the gloomy scene beyond.

'It would be most concerning if the weather delayed my journey to Cornwall tomorrow. I have a meeting with a potential client at a place called *Jamaica Inn*,' Pezzola muttered, looking nervously at the increasingly dire weather.

'You don't spend much time on the railways in England, I gather?' Mckelvie smiled.

'Why no…is it *inaffidbile*?' he asked, using his native tongue, before the confused look etched on his travel companion's face forced him to translate … 'how you say, *unreel'iable*?'

Mckelvie chuckled at the Italian's pronunciation once more.

'Unreliable is perhaps a fair word when the weather is a miss like this. Our trains struggle in extremes of weather!'

Pezzola afforded himself another hearty laugh despite the rather dire situation his travel plans found themselves in.

'It seems odd to me a country with such diverse weather can fail to plan ahead and suffer so greatly!'

'That, my dear fellow, is one of life's great mysteries!' Mckelvie mused.

'You say your business here is the passing of a client signor Mckelvie?' Pezzola asked, his tone more solemn.

'Yes, afraid so. He lived a full life though, all any of us can ask for, I suppose!'

'Ah si, it is the hope of us all to have a life that is most fulfilling.'

'Indeed, it is, and Lord Avery certainly had a fulfilling life by all accounts!' Mckelvie marvelled.

Giuseppe Pezzola's eyebrows rose at the mention of the name, his mouth falling open.

'Lord Avery you say? He is … was your client?'

'Why, yes,' Mckelvie started, confused: 'Did you know his lordship? I do hope I haven't broken such dreadful news to you?'

'No, no, I was not acquainted with his Lordship but his name, it is known to me yes. You see, I once worked closely with a nephew of his, a Meester Richard Haymer.'

'Richard? I say what an extraordinary coincidence! You'll no doubt be delighted to reacquaint yourself with him then – I've had word he is arriving back in Oakford today as well!' Mckelvie offered warmly.

Once more, Pezzola's expression changed. A grave confusion filled his face at the mention of Richard Haymer's impending presence in Oakford. Almost stunned, he remained silent before a concerned Mckelvie continued: 'I say, is everything OK, Mr Pezzola? You look as if you've seen a ghost!'

'Huh? Oh, sincerest apologies signor! I was, as your countryman would say, '*miles away*'. I am quite amazed to hear signor Haymer is here! It is, as you say, an extraordinary coincidence!'

'Yes, I bet it is! How long is it since you've last seen him?'

'It must be some years now. I would be most intrigued to meet with him once more,' Pezzola replied.

'Well perhaps you'll have a chance before your onward journey! Isn't it fascinating how these coincidences can occur?'

'Yes, most fascinating,' Pezzola said, his gaze drifting once more out of the window and to the windswept English countryside beyond, before changing the subject: 'Are there any sights one must see in Oak-Food, signor Mckelvie?'

'Well, if you are hoping for comparisons to the delights of Venice or Rome, I suspect you'll be sorely disappointed,' Mckelvie chuckled to himself. 'But the church is a rather beautiful example of early Victorian design! Other than that, it's the countryside herself out here that's the main draw.'

'Ah, grazie signor! But I suspect she is a countryside who isn't too welcoming to visit in weather such as this, eh!'

They both laughed heartily as the train began a slow descent into the small idyllic station of Oakford. For Mckelvie, the journey had proven rather delightful thanks in no small part to his travel companion. But something about Giuseppe Pezzola's presence in such a place niggled him, and he couldn't quite put his finger on it.

For Giuseppe Pezzola, the journey had been enlightening. His time in Oakford would perhaps not be as boring as he first suspected.

CHAPTER SEVEN

Wouldn't Mrs Farley like to know

Dr. Carson made his way to the village inn, the 'Hind's Head', a traditional coaching house with a thatched roof, wood beamed, low ceilings and large open fireplaces, making it a firm favourite with the locals and the only inn for weary travellers making their way on to Cornwall. The inn had been run by the eccentric Mrs. Farley for the last 20 years, 15 of which had seen her as sole proprietor following the untimely demise of her husband in a hunting accident.

A charismatic old maid, Mrs Farley was in her mid-40's and yet her wiry brown curls, plump figure and rounded glasses made her seem at least a decade further gone. Hardly anything went on in the village of Oakford without her knowledge and it had long been known that she was the first point of call for anybody in need of information. She liked few things more than her evening tipple, but one thing would certainly be the opportunity to gossip.

As Dr. Carson walked the cobbled streets, past the old well and the post office, he tipped his hat politely at the passing villagers, noting their acknowledgment whilst ensuring he kept a strong pace. The air had a particular biting chill to it that morning and he was adamant that if snow was to fall that day as expected, it was surely to be a fair few inches overnight.

Finally, reaching the inn's aged oak door, he opened it and immediately felt the pull of the warmth from the hearty fireplaces brightly lit in the spacious, low beamed pub.

'Good morning doctor come in out of the cold. Mrs Farley, in her apron, welcomed him kindly as she continued to clean down the bar.

'Thank you, Mrs Farley, it is awfully brisk today – I should suspect we might finally get that snowstorm before too long.'

'Oh, I've no doubt doctor – I can always tell when snow's coming,' the landlady proudly stated, before continuing: 'Mr Mckelvie arrived about an hour ago. I can go and let him know of your arrival if you'd like?'

Dr Carson was taken aback. 'But how did you know I was here to see him? Did he tell you?'

A glint appeared in the landlady's eye, as she replied 'Not said a word to me, but who else would you be here to see – I can't imagine it's that foreign salesman who arrived at the same time? No, it must be Mr Mckelvie, especially on a day like today, what with old Lord Avery's will being read, God bless his soul.'

'Why, nobody knows about the will reading and least still my involvement.'

'Ah, but doctor, there's no such thing as a secret in these parts. I would have thought you'd realise that by now!' she chuckled to herself.

'Well, yes, but at any rate – that's information even YOU couldn't possibly know,' he replied offhandedly before his cheeks begun to turn a slight shade of crimson at his choice of phrasing, 'not that I mean you personally, of course, Mrs Farley!'

'Don't fret yourself doctor, there's nothing much left that can shock me after 20 years running this place! I am a wealth of information in this village and don't mind the labelling as a "nosey old spinster" as it's been said.'

'Well, I would hardly use such a term, Mrs Farley, but your powers of deduction certainly are much admired,' Dr Carson added, nervously pulling at his collar, keen to avoid offending his host.

At this moment, footsteps on the ancient staircase behind the bar interrupted the conversation and Mr. Mckelvie appeared in the doorway, sparing the doctor's blushes and ending the conversation prematurely.

'Morning, Doctor Carson, thank you for meeting me.'

'Not a problem at all, Mr Mckelvie. It has been some time since we've seen you in these parts. I trust your journey from London went well?'

'Yes, as a matter of fact, it proved most interesting! Shall we have a spot of tea and I'll fill you in before we need to head out?'

'Certainly,' Dr Carson agreed.

'Excellent! Mrs Farley would you be so kind as to rustle up some tea and perhaps a couple of scones, if it isn't too much trouble?' Mckelvie enquired as he directed the doctor to a quiet corner as far from the bar and the old spinster's prying ears as he could manage.

'Of course, sir' she replied, as he made his retreat, naturally disappointed that her tasks would take her out of earshot for what she assumed would be a most interesting piece of information to add to her repertoire. It was, after all, her forté to know when to listen, and something in Mr Mckelvie's voice suggested his train journey had been most interesting.

Once he was quite sure that the nosey landlady had departed to the kitchen, Mr Mckelvie hastily informed Doctor Carson of his conversation with Giuseppe Pezzola on the train ride.

'Well, that's quite an extraordinary coincidence if ever I've heard one,' the doctor exclaimed, his eyebrows raising in amazement.

'That's if it IS a coincidence, my dear fellow,' Mckelvie replied.

'You don't mean to say you think this Mr Pezzola's timing is deliberate?'

'Well, it seems rather unlikely that young Mr Haymer would reappear here after all these years and it just so happens to be at the exact same time as an old business acquaintance from the continent turns up?!'

'Yes, when you put it like that it does seem rather far-fetched'

'Pezzola is certainly...'

Mrs Farley reappeared almost silently, stopping the conversation abruptly as both men seemed quite surprised with the stealthy way she had entered the nook without so much as a groan from the oak panelling under foot.

'Ah, wonderful! Nothing quite beats a good cup of tea on a cold day, I must say.' Mckelvie was the first to talk, eager to break the obvious silence.

'Warms the cockles, that's what my old mum used to say when I was a young girl,' Mrs Farley agreed, seemingly oblivious to the two men's awkwardness.

'Yes, quite so! Thank you very much Mrs Farley, you are a hostess of superb skills,' Mckelvie bowed his head perhaps just a little too low as he attempted to charm the landlady.

Doctor Carson was better acquainted with the wily old maid and suspected his colleague's attempts at avoiding her suspicions would only serve to arouse them further. As she made her leave, the subtle smile on her face suggested his assumptions were close to the mark.

'So, what do you say then, Mr Mckelvie? Should we confront Mr Haymer?'

'And say what, dear doctor? We have met an old acquaintance and suspect there to be an ulterior motive to his being here! It wouldn't wash! Travelling salesmen, after all, DO travel.'

'You make a valid point, but it does sound awfully fishy.'

'My thoughts exactly. As we are to be unwitting observers in the family affairs this weekend, I suggest we keep our eyes firmly peeled, and if Mr

Haymer does appear at odds, then we can determine our next course of action!'

Doctor Carson nodded his head in agreement. Perhaps this weekend would turn out to be more entertaining than he had previously suspected. 'Undercover detectives? I'm game! If Mr Pezzola is here to meet with his old friend, then having you staying here will certainly help us with our little investigation.'

'Well, one thing's for sure – if we do need to know about any of his movements, we need only engage Mrs Farley in the conversation and I suspect we will have every detail right down to the amount of chews it took him to finish off his lamb chop at dinner!' Mckelvie interjected lightheartedly.

They both laughed at the amusing image of Mrs Farley documenting each 'chew' from her vantage point behind the old wooden bar as they finished their teas and scones in high spirits.

❋ ❋ ❋

As they finally bade their hostess farewell, Mr Mckelvie instructed Mrs Farley he wouldn't be in need of dining arrangements that evening. The two men wrapped up in their large overcoats, then made their way into the sleeting rain outside, which was fast becoming snow.

As the oak door closed heavily behind them, the howling wind silenced and the glowing fire restored warmth to the ancient, empty bar. Mrs Farley stood, as she always did, behind the ale pumps, watching on as the two figures disappeared in the sleet beyond the old windows. Despite her best efforts, she hadn't managed to hear much of their conversation at all as she approached with their tea. But she had heard the name 'Pezzola' and couldn't help but wonder how the small Italian salesman had been of such interest to the solicitor and doctor. She certainly didn't have the faintest idea. 'Yet', she said out loud to herself, she didn't have the faintest idea 'yet'. It was surely only a matter of time, for there was nothing happening in Oakford that she couldn't find out.

CHAPTER EIGHT

The beauty of being an Avery

The fire in the library roared, lighting the room as the wood crackled fiercely. Gerald Avery stood alongside the fireplace hearth, resting his elbow on the mantel, whisky in hand as he stared forlornly at the large painting of his father staring down at him from on high.

Theirs had often been a fractious relationship over the years, much of which stemmed from his father's insistence that his son follow in his footsteps and become Lord of Oakford. It was a subject that had often caused them to fall out for days at a time. It wasn't that he wouldn't become Lord Avery; the title held great appeal, especially amongst his friends in London. It was his reluctance to move permanently back to

Oakford Court and oversee the estate that so infuriated his late father.

But Gerald Avery had long felt there was more to life than the curtain twitching antics of the villagers. A point that had been driven home to him when he left the sleepy countryside setting for the first time and moved, just a few short years earlier, to the bright lights of London. It was his insistence that he could maintain his city life even as eventual Lord of Oakford that had led to a deep rift in his relationship with his father that had never healed.

Just then the door opened and in came his cousins, Richard Haymer and Lillie Morris.

'Ah, there you are Gerry, old boy, on the hard stuff already I see!' Haymer quipped merrily.

Gerald eyed his cousins as they moved into the room and over to the drinks trolley, where Haymer began to fill two tumblers.

Whilst they had grown up together, Gerald had always resented his cousin's easy-natured life and the way his own parents doted on their nephew more than him. When Richard had announced he was off to the continent on an expedition which was nothing short of a jolly, it was met with warm encouragement from Lord Avery, a far cry from the reaction he had gotten when informing his father he wanted to move to the city to pursue a career on his own merit.

'Accountant? What sort of life choice is that for a member of the gentry? Why can't you travel like your cousin Richard – broaden the mind with experience not numbers!' the late Lord had barked, his words still clear in Gerald's head.

'Another tipple, Gerry?' Haymer's voice bringing his focus back to the room.

'I might as well. It is soon to be my whisky, after all!' he replied dryly.

The other two laughed at the comment as they all took seats beside the fire and raised a glass in a toast led by Richard Haymer.

'Well, here's to Uncle Dickie, a truly remarkable man!'

'Here, here!' Lillie agreed as they all took a sip.

'And, of course, here's to the new Lord Avery of Oakford, dear cousin Gerald,' Haymer announced once more.

The all took another sip before Gerald responded.

'Lord Avery, pah! A title or a prison sentence, I'm not quite sure which.'

'Oh, come now, Gerald, it surely isn't all that bad?' Lillie offered.

'To be a Lord of such an estate is an honour, dear boy,' Haymer announced, admiring the grandeur around them.

Gerald frowned at the comment, it was most peculiar to him.

'A rather rich statement coming from you, wouldn't you say Richie?'

'How so?'

'Well, you've always maintained that being trapped here in this village would be nothing short of a curse.'

Richard Haymer seemed to shift in his seat, taking a gulp of his whisky before laughing in his easy manner.

'Perhaps it's the many years on the continent that makes one appreciate the comforts of home, I suppose!'

'Yes, perhaps so,' Gerald replied, the frown remaining.

'I'm sure you'll find your way once the title is yours, Gerald, all you can do is your best,' Lillie said, sympathetically.

The three of them sat for a moment in an awkward silence, nobody sure what to say next. Gerald fingered his glass tentatively, his thoughts far from the mundane world of Oakford.

'One thing is for certain, it is only a matter of hours now till the future of our illustrious family is mapped out for us, whether we concur or not. The beauty of being an Avery!'

He downed the remnants of his whiskey and looked up once more at the imposing figure of his father looming large from upon high.

They may have all found different ways into the Avery tapestry, but each of them could relate to the sentiment. Named as such or not, an Avery was expected to perform a role, a role which persisted for life.

Once more, silence overcame the room.

CHAPTER NINE

A party...of sorts

The conditions had worsened still by the time Lady Avery's chauffeur Conroy arrived in Oakford village to collect Dr Carson and Mr Mckelvie. The two men were grateful for the comforts of the automobile as neither man fancied the long 3-mile trek in weather as bitterly cold as this.

Conroy was a non-descript sort of servant, his black uniform somewhat creased and his cap pulled low to conceal much of his face as he dutifully nodded to both men as they entered the vehicle, closing the door behind them and making his way back to the driver's seat.

The journey to Oakford Court would normally take just 10 minutes in the car and yet, on this occasion, the treacherous, icy roads slowed progress down to nearer 25 minutes. When they finally caught a glimpse of the large cast iron gates appearing ahead of them, it was fair to say both men and the normally impassive driver were relieved in equal measure. The tree-lined avenue swayed in the strong winds and Doctor Carson couldn't help but think back to a few days previously when he had last made this journey late into the evening. Despite it only being mid-afternoon now, the dark skies and the wail of the wind left him just as uneasy as before. It was as if the old court was issuing a foreboding warning to its latest guests, willing them to turn round, back to the safety of Oakford.

Doctor Carson shuddered at the ludicrous thought in his mind and focused his attention on the grand gravel driveway appearing ahead. Despite the weather and his own trepidations, the grand entrance and first reveal of the old mansion never ceased to take his breathe away.

As they came to a stop as close to the large-panelled doors as possible, Conroy braved the storm to open the passenger door and helped his two guests out of the vehicle. As if by clockwork, Harley appeared at the exact same moment, opening the exterior doors, and ushering the two men through into the sanctuary of the entrance hall.

'Welcome, gentleman, may I take your coats,' Harley enquired once the wailing storm outside had been shut out of the room.

'Thank you, Harley, it is simply awful out there,' Doctor Carson said, shaking off his soaked overcoat.

'May I suggest you go through to the library gentleman and warm yourselves by the fire?'

'It may take a little more than a fire to warm us up after that journey,' quipped Mr Mckelvie, rubbing his arms to relieve the cold.

'Perhaps a cognac would suffice, sir,' Harley replied, his monotone voice hiding the wit with effortless ease.

'You always know exactly what works, Harley, I do enjoy visiting a house with such an efficient butler,' Mr Mckelvie replied, chuckling.

'You're too kind, sir,' Harley replied. 'If you'd like to follow me, gentlemen.'

Entering the library, the two men were served a glass of cognac each and left alone.

'It's really quite an impressive pile this isn't it,' Mckelvie marvelled, admiring the ornate wood carving of the fireplace.

'I've always found it quite fascinating – certainly more extravagant than most of my other house visits.'

'Yes, I suppose so,' Mckelvie nodded, although his line of work was varied, unlike the doctor, and he had many a client with similar properties to Oakford Court.

As they continued their mutual admiration of the building's interior craftsmanship, the library door flung open and in came Gerald Avery.

'Dr Carson, it's good to see you again.' He approached the doctor, shaking his hand vigorously.

'Gerald, how are you? You remember your father's solicitor, Mr Mckelvie?'

'Yes, yes. Mr Mckelvie, thank you for coming so promptly. I know mother is keen to put this business to bed and so am I,' he uttered, shaking the older man's hand.

'Certainly so, Mr Avery. I was very sorry to hear about your father's passing. He was a great man and one I always enjoyed meeting over the long years I knew him,' Mckelvie reflected solemnly.

'Indeed, he was,' Gerald replied before continuing rather quickly 'but such is the nature of life! He certainly wouldn't want us dwelling on the past.'

'How is your mother, Gerald?' Doctor Carson continued.

'Oh, you know mother, a pure battle-axe made of steel. It would take more than mere death to dampen her spirits!'

'She is certainly an impressive lady.'

Gerald helped himself to a drink and changed his focus to Mr Mckelvie.

'Mother informs me we are to have the will reading following dinner this evening, Mr Mckelvie. I trust most arrangements will be in place for everything to be handled with sensitivity?'

'Of course, Mr Avery, we are experts in discretion, and I assure you all details are in place to ensure your father's wishes have been catered for to the letter.'

'Quite, quite. Thank you, Mr Mckelvie, it is most reassuring to hear so.' Gerald Avery, though, seemed much less assured than his statement would suggest.

At that moment they were all interrupted by the arrival of Richard Haymer and Lillie, laughing between themselves as they entered the room.

'Oh, pardon us chaps! Didn't realise the party had started already,' Haymer quipped in a jovial tone.

'It's hardly appropriate to call it a party, Haymer,' Gerald scolded.

'Well come now, Gerald, it's snowing, we have all the family together and now guests! I'd say it merits a party and I dare say dear old Uncle Dickie would want it to be so,' Haymer replied heartily to his cousin, dismissing his strong glare.

Shaking hands warmly with both Doctor Carson and Mr Mckelvie before introducing Lillie to both, Haymer, as he often did, became the sole focus of the room as he continued: 'Can I interest anyone in a smoke? Deathly cold out there and I, for one, am not a fan of it!'

He shared his cigarettes with Lillie, Mr Mckelvie and Gerald, before turning to the Dr Carson.

'One for you, doctor?'

'No, thank you, Mr Haymer, I am not a smoker.'

'A doctor who doesn't smoke?!' Haymer exclaimed! 'Well, that is a first! I assumed it was a mandatory obligation'

'I do make up a minority, you are quite right about that!'

'Well, suit yourself! Each to their own and all that,' Haymer continued, striking a match to light his cigarette.

The group chatted warmly and for the first time in a long time, the old house felt truly like an inviting home. The roaring fire was well stocked up and the group joined in a card game, all in good spirits, all oblivious to the snowstorm which was finally and firmly falling in earnest outside.

CHAPTER TEN

Lord Avery – The Will

At 7pm, the group moved to the dining room and took their seats at the long wooden dining table. It was neatly laid out with cutlery, plates, glasses, and exquisite candelabras offering a dim glow which complimented the room's low lighting.

Lady Avery and the Colonel had joined the others as they entered the room, whilst Mrs Langtry had sufficiently overcome her earlier ills to join the party shortly thereafter, her pale disposition suggesting she wasn't quite her old self.

The dinner had started in good spirit with much of the conversation between the group focused on current affairs and memories of days gone by. The continuing decline in weather was also on most people's minds.

'It really is going to be quite a challenge this weather,' Mrs Langtry murmured, looking at the increasingly heavy snowfall building outside the window.

'Not had snow like this since I was a boy,' the Colonel huffed.

'We must ensure we don't leave it too late to venture back to the village, Mckelvie,' Doctor Carson said across the table to the solicitor, who had been placed next to the delightful Lillie.

'Oh, surely you can't go out in this weather! It's simply dreadful,' Lillie cried out.

'Yes, don't be daft chaps, unless you have bought skis with you, I hardly imagine you'd make it back!' Haymer interjected.

'I'm sure we will be fine, it's a route I've taken hundreds of times before.'

'Nonsense, doctor, Richard is quite right. It's not wise to risk this weather. You shall both spend the night here, I'll have Harley make arrangements,' Lady Avery stated in a definitive tone as she rang the service bell.

The old butler arrived at her side almost instantly, appearing in the room without any of the guests noticing his arrival.

'You rang, m'lady?'

'Ah Harley, Mr Mckelvie and the doctor will be staying here tonight to see out this dreadful storm, so please prepare rooms for each of them. And whilst you're at it, could you please ring Mrs Farley at the Hind's Head and inform her not to expect Mr Mckelvie back till tomorrow?'

'Right away, my lady, will that be all?'

'For now, yes, thank you. Though please do let the maids know we will take tea in the sitting room whilst the will is seen to.'

'Of course, ma'am', he bowed his head and disappeared almost as effortlessly as he arrived.

'That's awfully kind of you, Lady Avery, thank you,' Mr Mckelvie said, grateful that they wouldn't have to face the extremes of the cold weather once more, today at least.

'No need for gratitude, Mr Mckelvie, it would be most criminal of me to let you leave in such conditions.'

'It's all very exciting,' Lillie squealed, 'being snowed in. I mean, it's quite the little adventure.'

'Met a chap once in India who told me a tale of a group snowed in up in the Himalayas – they were delirious from the cold and starving, so much so they resorted to cannibalism!' the Colonel exclaimed.

'Oh, how awful,' Mrs Langtry bemoaned.

'Wouldn't worry too much, Colonel, we have enough food here to last us a few weeks before we would have to resort to that!' Haymer announced, gaining light laughter from his dining partners.

Talk of the weather rumbled on as they finished their meals and slowly made their way into the sitting room for the reading of the last will and testament of Lord William Avery.

※ ※ ※

As they each took their seats in the sitting room, adjacent to the library, Mckelvie prepared his notes. The room had a high ceiling with a singular oriental chandelier hanging down, providing a dim glow across the variety of landscape paintings which adorned the walls. Another magnificent wood carved fireplace took centre stage, and it was in front of this that Mr Mckelvie found himself standing before his audience, evenly spread in a semi-circle of chairs and sofas around him.

He had done hundreds of will readings over the years and despite his vast experience, he always felt a sense of nervousness when addressing the grieving relatives of the deceased. Tonight, though, what struck him most wasn't the wave of emotion but rather the apparent lack of it. His audience looked on, not with a sense of loss but with a sense of expectation, each one almost excited at the news to come.

'Right then, as you are all aware, I am here on behalf of the firm Reed's, Mckelvie and Reed's as the solicitor and executor of the last will and testament of Lord William Richard Avery. He stipulated that all of you be present here during this reading as beneficiaries of his estate.' He paused for a moment, observing the faces staring intently back.

'Doctor Carson, as Lord Avery's long-term physician, was instructed as executor and witness of this will and has kindly agreed to join us.'

The doctor nodded a gentle acknowledgement of thanks to his fellow executor.

'Without further ado then, I shall read the will which Lord Avery made in my firm's offices in Knightsbridge on the 20th June 1931.'

'For my loyal servants Harley and Kumba, I leave £100 remunerations each as a thank you for their ongoing commitment to me and my wife.'

'For my siblings, dear brother Philip and sister Celia, I leave a sum of £5,000 each to be enjoyed as they see fit in their twilight years.'

Mrs Langtry had a small tear in her eyes at the news, a sum which would significantly ease her money troubles. The Colonel seemed uninterested in the news but nodded politely all the same.

'To my only nephew, Richard, I also leave my late brother's share of £5,000 to be made immediately available to him.'

'I say, that's awfully kind dear uncle,' Haymer exclaimed out loud. Lady Avery smiled kindly at her nephew's gratitude.

'Oakford Court and its possessions, I bequeath to my wife and my first-born son. The estate is to be preserved and passed down the male bloodline as it has for generations.'

Gerald smiled at the news whilst Lady Avery maintained her composure.

Mr Mckelvie concluded the reading and stipulated that each beneficiary would receive their entitlement in due course. The room was, as a whole, in good spirits and Gerald, of all people, leaped from his chair and exclaimed: 'Well then, as that's all been concluded what say we have a drink and play some cards?' his usually droll voice much brighter.

'If I didn't know better, I'd say you were starting a party Gerald? Hardly appropriate?' Haymer seized the opportunity to reuse his cousin's earlier comment against him in jest.

It took Gerald a second to understand the connection, but his good mood couldn't be altered.

'Oh yes, well now the formalities are over, I see no harm in us enjoying the rest of the evening.'

'Indeed, I'm sure you don't,' Haymer chuckled. 'Well, I'm game! Lillie?'

'Oh, yes, I've always fancied myself as quite the card shark,' she teased.

'Splendid! Doctor? Colonel? Care to join?'

'Well, why not!' Doctor Carson beamed.

'Yes, I don't see any harm in a quick flutter,' the Colonel concurred.

Lady Avery, Mrs Langtry and Mr Mckelvie opted for the more tranquil setting of the drawing room, whilst the rest of the party moved back to the Library to begin their card game.

The group had enjoyed two hands of Rummy before conversation turned to the preceding events of the evening.

'I suppose you'll have some plans for this place now you're the Lord of the Manor, Gerald?' Lillie said in her nonchalant sort of way.

'Oh, I'll have changes to be made that's for sure.'

'Not a fan of the décor, dear boy? I suppose you'll be able to kick the accounting job now though and dedicate some time to the change,' Haymer laughed, lighting another cigarette.

'What gives you that impression?' Gerald replied curtly.

'No offence intended. I just mean you'll be focusing on the estate now! It's the job of the heir incumbent.'

'I'm not going to be the dutiful son, sitting in this decrepit old crypt until the grim reaper comes knocking. No, things will be changing soon enough.' His tone was assured, as if he had long since come to this conclusion.

'You intend to stay in London Gerald?' Doctor Carson enquired.

'My life is in London now, it's where I belong.'

'And what of your commitments here? Oakford Manor needs to be maintained.' the Colonel was rarely a man who got worked up, but he seemed positively irate at his nephew's apparent lack of dedication to his duty.

'Mother is here and will stay here till the end, after which time I cannot say I intend to maintain the Manor.'

An uneasy silence fell over the group with that statement, none of them seemed quite sure how to continue.

'Well, Uncle Dickie was a good man and I only hope his legacy lives on,' Haymer said.

'Here, here. I doubt my sister-in-law will be enamoured with your plans, young man,' the Colonel continued, still irate with Gerald's blasé attitude.

'I agree, Colonel, I don't suppose dear mother would be, but such is life,' Gerald grinned.

The game continued with less amicable tones than before and Doctor Carson couldn't help but find his thoughts wandering back to his final conversation with Lord Avery. Had the old man known of his son's lack of commitment to the estate? If so, why hadn't he changed the will? Something was certainly not quite right with the situation.

As his thoughts returned to the game at hand, however, little did the doctor know that things were certainly not right – in fact, they were about to get a whole lot worse.

* * *

By 11pm, the collective group had retired for the evening. The snow outside had only gotten worse as the night had drawn in and there was now nearly 9 inches of snowfall in the low valleys surrounding Oakford.

The Court was quiet, tall dark shadows flung themselves from the large-panelled windows onto the wooden floor below. Doctor Carson had drifted off to sleep shortly before midnight, his thoughts troubled by the card game and the entire affair. His dreams caused him to toss and turn, before a loud thud made him awaken, startled.

Bolting up in his bed, he wiped the beads of sweat from his forehead and reached for his pocket watch on the bedside table. Squinting in the darkness, he just about made out the time, 1.20am. He was sure he had heard a loud thud. It couldn't have been his dreams so vividly, surely?

For a few moments, he sat upright, listening intently for a sound in the silence. He was just about to put it down to paranoia when the sound of footsteps pacing quickly down the corridor alerted him once more.

He certainly hadn't misheard that, the unmistakable creak of one of the floorboards suggested somebody was moving around the first-floor landing. As quickly as they had come, the sound of the footsteps disappeared, returning the Court to a state of utter silence once more. As the minutes passed, Doctor Carson found himself falling slowly into a deep sleep, but this time he dreamt of happier things.

CHAPTER ELEVEN

Death comes to us all

The next morning, Doctor Carson awoke to a ray of sunlight across his face. It was cold, and even as he slowly gained consciousness, he could feel the chill of the large grand room circling around him.

He had been given a pair of pyjamas and a robe the night before by the meticulous Harley and he reached for the robe now, grateful for the butler's thoughtfulness. As he got up, he stretched and yawned loudly as he went over to the large windows.

Drawing back the curtains, he was amazed by the blanket of white which had engulfed the long lawns below. Where yesterday he could make out the pathway leading down to the lake and the terraced patio, now he could see nothing but trees through the dense carpet of snow. Mercifully, it had ceased snowing during the night, but the extent of its severity was evident. It might be another day before the roads were driveable and he suspected the valley pass would be even more immersed than the estate's grounds.

Just then, he heard a loud piercing scream from the corridor beyond his room. Hurriedly tying his robe, he rushed to the door. As he flung it open, he nearly collided with Mr Mckelvie, who had just gone to knock on the door but had instead very nearly flown through it.

'What the devil is going on?!' Carson exclaimed.

'It's that young maid, she is in hysterics saying all sort of things,' Mckelvie started, out of breath. 'Something about young Mr Avery.'

With that, the two men made their way hastily down the corridor, turning the corner and finding themselves at the doorway of Gerald's room. The young maid was sat in the arms of Kumba, her head buried on the elder housekeeper's shoulder, sobbing uncontrollably.

'What is going on?' Doctor Carson asked of nobody in particular.

'It's Mr Gerald,' Kumba said in a state of shock.

Without another word, both men steeled themselves and moved into the bedroom. The odd-shaped corner room meant that they first came to a seating area which faced a large window overlooking the distant lake.

Turning to their right, a wooden step led up to the bedroom, where a four-poster bed sat central to a grand panelled wall. Mr Mckelvie saw it first.

'Oh, dear god' he uttered, his complexion paling as his wrinkled face widened in shock.

Laying on the bed was Gerald Avery, a large dagger protruding from a bloodied hole in his chest, his dead eyes wide open in a sense of terror.

*

Doctor Carson had seen many a dead body during his professional years but seldom came across a murder and certainly never a murder of someone who just twelve hours ago he had been conversing with.

His head was spinning wildly as he forced himself to undertake his professional obligations, searching for signs of life before making a preliminary scan of the body. He ascertained that Gerald couldn't have been dead any longer than 6 hours and as the time now was a little after 7am that would put the murder at any time between 1 and 2am.

Then he felt a chill down his spine as he recalled the events which had awoken him earlier in the night. Had it not been 1.20am when he checked his pocket watch? The sound of the footprints he had heard walking past his room could quite easily have been coming from the direction of Gerald's room. Had he heard the murderer making their retreat?! He cursed his laziness under his breath and swore to himself that he would relay this information to the police as soon as he possibly could.

Realising that there was no more he could do and that any further investigation could hamper the police when they arrived, he turned away from the stiff body and guided Mr Mckelvie back out of the room.

'We must phone the police at once,' he informed his shocked friend.

'Well yes, surely a murderer couldn't have got far in this weather!' Mckelvie spoke.

'That's if they've even left.'

'You mean to say they could still be here?!'

'Look at the snow, you know as well as I that it would have been simply impassable last night, not least without leaving a major trail – it's much more likely the killer is still here.'

'But that's, that's impossible! It means one

of the party from yesterday or one of the servants…'Mckelvie's voice trailed off, his years of experience in the world had never prepared him for the grim realities of murder.

'Let's not create more panic than necessary right now. We must call the police and take their advice, but first we must find out what the maid knows.'

Before they left the room and its ghastly scene behind them, Mckelvie took one last look at the horror show they had stumbled across. 'That weapon is awfully unusual isn't it,' said Mr Mckelvie, noting the ornate pattern on the murder weapon's handle as it stood protruding from the wound.

'I should imagine it is one of Lord Avery's collection from his time in Africa. I'm sure Harley will be able to tell us in due course.'

The two men nodded their agreement and left the room, moving over to the bench where the young maid had finally ceased sobbing, her eyes red and puffy from the strain as she sat quietly and visibly shaken. Kumba calmly held the girl as both sat in silence.

McKelvie, having restored his usual level of clarity, took the lead as he approached the young maid, crouching down alongside her to meet her face-to-face.

'I'm sorry to have to ask you this, young lady, but you understand the importance of sourcing the facts,' he said softly.

'Oh, sir, you can't think I've anything to do with it?!' she wailed, close to tears once more.

'Now, my dear girl, not at all. We simply need to know the facts of how you came to find ... the body.'

She grimaced at the word but began to calm as the fear of suspicion subsided.

'Was the door locked when you first arrived?' Doctor Carson interjected.

'It was, sir – Mr Avery, he asked me to wake him early this morning so he could go for a walk. The master always liked to walk in the winter, said the fresh air was good for the health....' She faded off, grasping at the tear dampened tissue she held tightly in her hand.

'And what time was that?'

'It was 6.30am, sir – I know because I had just passed the old grandfather clock on the ground floor as it chimed.'

Mckelvie nodded thoughtfully, 'And so you knocked, then tried the handle?'

'That's right, sir – I knocked and called out. When I heard no reply, I tried the handle and when I discovered it was locked, I wasn't sure what to do,' she exclaimed. 'I knew the master had been adamant I must wake him, so I pulled out my key and unlocked the door. I entered the room and called out again.'

'And that's when you found him?'

'I've never seen anything so horrifying in my whole life. His, his eyes were wide open – I don't think I'll ever forget that look,' she quivered.

'There, there, you have had a frightful shock,' Mckelvie said tenderly.

'Did you touch anything or move anything?' Doctor Carson asked abruptly.

'Sir?'

'Once you found the body – did you touch anything?'

'Why, no sir, certainly not. I was frozen still with fear. I just screamed out and rushed from the room.'

'That is when I came and found her out here, trembling and wailing,' Kumba spoke up, gently hugging the young maid.

'Yes, quite – well it's been an awful shock for us all. May I suggest you take the young girl and get her a strong drink to try and steady her nerves? We can oversee things from here.'

With that, Kumba took the young maid down the stairs and, for a moment, the two men were left in a silent state of shock. Before either could take the conversation further, they were joined in the hallway by Harley, who, if he knew much of the incredible events of the last hour, seemed as utterly calm as usual.

'Gentlemen, I ought to let you know that I have telephoned the Chief Inspector and he has informed me that he will be here as soon as the weather allows.'

'Right, good job Harley. When did you hear of what's happened?! Have you spoken to any of the other guests?' Mckelvie enquired.

'I heard the commotion with the maid this morning and as I was on my way down the corridor, I arrived just after Kumba,' the butler started, his tone hardly changing an octave. 'Once it was apparent what had happened to the master, I felt it imperative to call the police at once.'

'Yes, quite so,' Mckelvie nodded, 'but you didn't actually enter the room yourself?'

The old butler steeled himself, showing the first signs of humanity, but only briefly, before composing his thoughts and replying as calmly as ever. 'No, sir, I suppose the need to do so didn't cross my mind – after all, the maid's hysteria was evidence enough of what she'd discovered.'

'Well, I suppose there isn't anything else we can

do for now, Harley. Do you have a key on you for Mr Avery's room? It is a crime scene so we must lock it until the police arrive.'

'Of course, sir.' With that, he locked the door and turned back to the two gentlemen.

'Is there anything else you need gentlemen? I ought to be ensuring breakfast is served.'

'That will do for now, Harley,' Doctor Carson interjected. 'It would be best if I spoke to Lady Avery, she is certain to have a tremendous shock losing her son so soon after her husband.'

'Indeed, sir. Her ladyship usually stays in her room until breakfast. Shall I ask her to meet you downstairs?'

'Thank you, Harley.'

He nodded and, as quietly as he had appeared, he was gone.

'Well, that was awfully odd,' Mckelvie uttered when they were once again alone.

'What was?' Doctor Carson asked, unsure of what his colleague meant.

'Harley's expression when I asked him if he had been in the room. Seemed a bit surprised to me.'

'Yes, I suppose he did. More than that, when I said about Lady Avery, there was something in his tone that …oh I don't know…'

'No, you're not wrong, my dear boy, I noticed it too – he seemed almost humoured by the suggestion it would be a terrible shock for Lady Avery to learn of her son's death,' Mckelvie suggested

'Yes, that's exactly it – most odd indeed. I am not sure we can be too careful with all this. We must ensure we get the opportunity to speak to the Chief Inspector when he arrives. There is also one other thing…'

'What is it?'

'Last night, I awoke around 1.20am to the sound of a loud thud. I know that's the right time as I checked my pocket watch. At first, I thought I must have dreamt it but then, shortly after, I heard footsteps outside the door. They were coming from this direction and moving quickly.'

'Well I say!' Mckelvie was astounded. 'You mean to suggest you heard the murderer?!'

'It seems incredulous, but yes, the time fits with my examination of the body.'

'Well then your right we really mustn't waste any time in talking to the Chief Inspector.'

'Quite so, Mckelvie, we must assume that one or more of our fellow guests knows more than they will let on.'

Mr Mckelvie nodded in agreement but was

clearly unsettled by the thought.

Doctor Carson continued: 'I will now go and speak to Lady Avery but keep your wits about you whilst I'm gone…. there's a murderer in our midst.'

CHAPTER TWELVE

A mother always knows

Lady Avery took the news with the grace and elegance one would expect from a lady of her standing. Doctor Carson, though, had broken such news to family members before and saw enough in her old, wise eyes to know the true devastation that had befallen her, despite her exterior calmness.

She had taken a few moments to compose herself upon hearing the news of her son, and in her silence, he suspected she was trying hard not to allow herself to cry in his presence. She was nothing if not an exceptionally proud woman.

Without going into too much detail, he told

her of the events that had unfolded in the early hours of that morning and assured her that the police would be along soon to take charge and investigate. He left out the information about his late-night experience and his suspicion of his fellow guests.

'I suspect you think it is one of the guests,' Lady Avery stated calmly.

Doctor Carson was taken aback: 'Why, what makes you say that!'

'Come now, doctor, I may be an old widower dealing with a sudden and devastating shock, but I am also no fool.'

'No, you're certainly not. Yes, Lady Avery if you must know, I suspect your son's death is likely to have been caused by someone from within the house. The storm, you see, was just too severe last night for an outsider to get in and out without being noticed.'

'My son wanted rid of this house. Do you suppose that could be the cause of all this?'

Again, the doctor was gobsmacked. Surely the old lady couldn't have known of her son's plans?! He had only announced them carelessly the night before and she had long since retired to bed.

'But how...'

'How did I know of Gerald's plans?

'Well, yes.'

'A mother always knows dear doctor. Gerald had never warmed to this house. He hated the idea of being cooped up and responsible for its upkeep. Dickie and he would row over it relentlessly, because my husband simply could not understand why he wouldn't want to fulfil his family legacy.'

'And yet, he left Gerald the house regardless?'

'He was a stickler for family tradition and the Avery tradition has always been estates to be left to the first-born son.'

Doctor Carson found himself thinking once more about his conversation with Lord Avery. Perhaps the lord knew his son was likely to want the place gone as soon as he inherited it, and that's why he made the doctor swear to the most unusual task of helping keep the house safe. Not that he could do very much! But desperation on the deathbed must be a great cause, he assumed, of such last wishes.

'Well?' Lady Avery brought him back to reality.

'Sorry, Lady Avery, you were saying?'

'Do you suppose my son's desire to sell the old place could have caused his death?'

'Oh, well yes I suppose it could be a possibility. We shouldn't really assume anything though, not until Inspector Boyle gets here.'

'He's a most competent Inspector - I am pleased he is personally taking charge of this, this nightmare,' she replied.

✽ ✽ ✽

The morning sunlight had mercifully started to melt the snow and whilst the roads remained near impassable due to the ice, the route cross-country was achievable for a determined rambler like Inspector Boyle.

In his late 50's, the Inspector was a man of average height and build with wavy brown hair and a crooked nose, best noted for his unique powers of deduction, which were known to be anything but ordinary. As a young officer he had excelled in London but had moved out to the country and into semi-retirement following his wife's illness a couple of years ago. Even so, he was soon gaining a strong reputation for solving even the most notoriously difficult of crimes and it was this talent which made his services continually requested by forces around the country.

As he hoisted his overcoat collar high to his ears and checked that his shoelaces were tied in multiples of four, an odd habit from childhood, he continued on over the hills and through the fresh winter morning air, and surmised – as he often did - that his choice of moving to the country had been a good one. London was far too congested and polluted, nothing quite like the air here. Good for the lungs!

One thing that had never ceased to fascinate him though was the criminal mind. When he left the London metropolis, he assumed his busiest tasks 'out in the sticks' would be solving mysteries around missing cows and petty theft from village shops. He never imagined that village life in the country could be quite so dark. Murder, it seemed, existed in even the most picturesque and peaceful of settings. In fact, more than just existing, he considered to himself, it seemed to positively thrive.

CHAPTER THIRTEEN

The stranger by the lake

Richard Haymer paced the sitting room restlessly, deep in thought as he tried to process the information that had just been shared at the end of breakfast.

'It just seems impossible,' he muttered, more to himself than anyone else.

'Oh, it's simply horrifying,' wailed Mrs Langtry. 'My brother and now my nephew – it's as if the family is cursed!'

'Now, really mother,' Lillie replied to her step-mother. 'You ought not to say such things!'

The three of them were joined in the room by Mr Mckelvie, who had opted to join the others at breakfast whilst the doctor spoke privately to Lady Avery. The Colonel had left following breakfast, opting to walk the grounds, as he often did.

'Inspector Boyle from the Oakford Constabulary is on his way, so, for now, all we can do is try and remain calm,' Mckelvie informed the others.

'Calm? That's a good joke, old boy! Hardly calming knowing there's been a murder in the house!' Haymer said in jest. His tone, though, suggested he was as nervous as Mrs Langtry.

'I can't stay in a house of murder,' Mrs Langtry announced. 'We shall return to Fowey as soon as the weather enables Lillie.'

Her stepdaughter seemed less eager to leave, Mckelvie thought, but nonetheless she dutifully nodded her agreement.

'I just can't understand why an intruder would kill Gerald,' Mrs Langtry continued.

Mckelvie noted both Lillie and Richard Haymer's reactions and suspected they were both thinking along the same lines as he, that it was more likely the murderer was still among the house party – and, if that was the case, none of them could feel truly safe until the killer was revealed.

❋ ❋ ❋

The fresh morning air did little to distract the Colonel as he walked, stick in hand, across the grounds of his ancestral estate. He always liked to walk this route when he stayed here. It reminded him of his childhood and of happy innocent times with his siblings.

The great redwoods that stood proudly a hundred feet above him blocked out the sun's glare as he made his way down to the water's edge. The lake itself was still frozen and bare, except for a few brave ducks walking on its now solid surface. Leaning slightly on his stick, he stopped and gathered his thoughts in peace.

It had been an extraordinary 24 hours and whilst he had never particularly warmed to his nephew, especially knowing his lack of respect for his birth right, his sudden and unexpected death had bought about new challenges. It occurred to the Colonel that he would now more than likely be inheriting the estate's and taking responsibility for its upkeep, something he hadn't really considered before as the third son. The death of his oldest brother had left Dickie to take the reins and, when he then bore a son, the Colonel had contented himself with a graceful life of leisure. His passion of travelling the colonies and exploring the countryside had kept him busy, and when he did return to Oakford each year, he was more than happy playing second fiddle to his sibling.

Now his dear brother had passed, and his son had perished, he would have to take on a full-time position at this late stage in his life. But he mustered his proud stiff upper lip and determined one must perform one's duty.

Just then, as he gazed absently across the lake, he caught a movement in the corner of his eye, off to the left where the trees were thicker and cornered the lakeside with forestry. At first, he had assumed it to be a deer or fox but, turning his head sharply, he was sure he had caught sight of a man's shadow.

'Who's there?' he bellowed, his breath wheezing as he called out into the cold morning air.

Whilst his eyesight wasn't as sharp as it once was, he managed to make out a figure with a dark, tanned complexion and greased black hair.

Before he could analyse the stranger any further, the shadowy figure disappeared off into the forest beyond, rustling leaves as they moved quickly from view.

'Bloody coward!' The Colonel called. 'Show yourself!'

The rustling faded and the tranquil peace of the frozen lake returned.

The Colonel suspected the shadowy figure may just be the man who had entered the house the night before and committed the heinous murder of his nephew.

'I must return at once to the house and speak to that Inspector whatshisname,' he declared out loud to himself. With that, he thrust his walking stick forward and marched with a renewed vigour back up the pathway leading through the trees to the distant house beyond.

CHAPTER FOURTEEN

The Inspector calls

Inspector Boyle found himself at Oakford Court in good time, his strong pace having put him in good stead across the snow-covered moors.

He had only visited the old house a couple of times before when he had dutifully attended gala dinners on behalf of the local police force, yet he was still amazed by the magnificent and imposing first impression the building gave. The gargoyles and turrets high above him, and the old flag tower with the family coat of arms embedded in the stone, both highlighted the history and stature of its occupants and, yet, there was something uninviting about the place – as if it wanted to be left well alone.

A queer thought, he uttered, shaking his head at his wild imagination as he made his way up to the grand front doors.

Harley, the old man servant, had the front door open on the first knock and was soon taking the Inspector's overcoat.

'Doctor Carson has requested your company in the library, Inspector. Shall I take you there first?'

'Carson's here? Well then, yes, thank you,' he replied, curious as to why the doctor was here and why he would specifically request his attention before he met Lady Avery and investigated the scene of the crime.

Harley opened the door of the library, allowed the Inspector to pass through and then closed the door with a gentle thud.

'Inspector Boyle! I am so glad you were able to get here so promptly,' the doctor said, shaking the Inspector's hand warmly. The two men had met on occasions through the requirements of their professions and Carson's general care for Mrs Boyle. For his part, Boyle had always liked the younger doctor's way and attitude.

'Doctor Carson, I must confess I'm surprised to see you here?'

'Oh, yes of course! I was here for dinner last

night as a witness to Lord Avery's will along with the family solicitor Mr Mckelvie, and with the weather taking a turn for the worse, we were kindly offered rooms. Although it's been quite a night!'

'Yes, it certainly sounds as if it has,' Boyle agreed, before asking: 'Tell me doctor, have you had a chance to examine the body?'

'Well yes, I was one of the first to arrive at the scene upon the discovery of poor old Gerald this morning and it's murder alright! Gerald Avery had been stabbed by a large ornate dagger, which I suspect is one from his lordship's collection.'

'I see, and who made the discovery?'

'A young maid by the name of Amy Sheldon, a mere child, really, and naturally very shaken by the whole turn of events! I tried to question her but couldn't get much more information than she had found the body just after 7am and had left the room straight after.'

'And would you say the murder had taken place shortly before this time?'

'Oh no, from the onset of rigour mortis, I would place the time of death at between 1 and 2am.'

'That's most helpful, Doctor Carson, most helpful!' Boyle chimed as he took notes in his small handheld notebook. 'I think I should now go and see the crime scene if there isn't anything else?'

'There is one thing Inspector....'

'Yes?'

'Well it may have no bearing whatsoever on the case, but you see the timing fits too well.'

'You have me intrigued doctor, do spit it out!'

'Yes, sorry! Only I was awoken by what sounded like a loud thud at approximately 1.20am last night. At first, I thought nothing of it but then I heard fast-paced footsteps along the corridor outside, coming from the direction of Gerald's room.'

'Well that certainly is interesting,' Boyle said, his head buried downwards as he scribbled furiously in his notebook.

'When I examined the body and realised the timing, it dawned on me that the person I heard in the night could very easily have been our murderer.'

'Yes, I dare say it probably was!' Boyle exclaimed; his brows raised as the possibility lodged itself deep in his thoughts. 'Does anyone else know of this, doctor?'

'Only Mr Mckelvie.'

'And you trust this solicitor?'

'Oh yes, Mr Mckelvie is a very honest and decent man.'

'That's good – but I think it best we keep this information between the three of us for now.'

'I quite agree, Inspector.'

'That's settled then, perhaps you could accompany me to see the body and then meet with Lady Avery?'

'Yes, of course, she was naturally very shocked at the news and has opted to remain in her own room ever since,' Doctor Carson informed the Inspector as they left the library and made their way back to the entrance hallway.

The large ornate staircase looked less intimidating in the morning light, its cast iron balustrades casting beautiful shadows across the wall beyond as the two men made their ascent to the first-floor landing.

Kumba appeared from one of the guest rooms with a feather duster and seemed startled by the appearance of the Inspector. He was as calm as ever and politely nodded his head at the maid as they passed.

'This is Gerald Avery's room,' Doctor Carson pointed as they arrived.

'Has it been locked since the discovery?'

'Yes, we had Kumba - the old housekeeper we just passed - lock it once I had concluded my initial examination earlier.'

'That was the right thing to do. Any evidence left behind by the killer could be crucial to solving this case,' Boyle stated before calling out to Kumba from the end of the corridor.

The old maid turned, positively concerned by the Inspector's request to see her, and made her way hastily to the two men.

'Ah, it's Kumba isn't it?' Boyle asked, looking at her with his expressionless eyes.

'Yes, sir.' She bowed her head slightly.

'Kumba, could you kindly open the door.'

'Of course, sir,' she dutifully responded, taking a key from her pinafore and slowly unlocking the large oak door, the sound of the latch releasing audible to all three of them.

'Thank you. Can you tell me who has a key to this room other than yourself?'

She paused for a second, her wrinkled face scrunching together as she thought hard.

'Mr Harley has one. He has the keys to every room and Lady Avery has a master key, but that one is always stored in her safe,' she stated. 'And, of course, Mr Gerald, he has…. had a key.'

'That's very helpful, thank you. I wonder if you can arrange for the young maid, Amy, isn't it, to join me downstairs later? Just as a matter of due diligence to confirm her account of this morning's events?'

'Certainly, Inspector, I will have her meet you once she has finished in the pantry,' Kumba replied, the exotic twang of her accent firmly distinct despite all her years in England.

'That would be perfect. I will need to also confirm your movements at some point,' he began, noting her eyes widening, before assuring her 'just as a matter of elimination.'

'Yes, of course, Inspector. I will be available when you need me,' she replied, the colour returning to her face as she turned and made her way back down the corridor.

'A peculiar woman that one,' Boyle observed, before turning his attention to the open door ahead of him.

As he entered Gerald Avery's bedroom, followed closely by the doctor, he observed the undisturbed lounge space with its chaise lounge displaying ruffled cushions and, alongside, an empty, used whisky glass sat on the coffee table. Turning his focus to the bedroom, he saw the body lying motionless atop of the sheets on the grand four-poster bed.

Doctor Carson gasped as he hurried past the Inspector and looked down at the stiff, pale corpse that was Gerald Avery.

'It's gone?!' he stammered. 'The dagger has gone!'

'Hang on a minute,' Inspector Boyle stated calmly, joining him at the side of the bed. 'You mean to tell me the dagger was left in situ when you left the room?'

'Yes! We left everything as we found it, ready for your arrival.'

The bloody wound on Gerald's chest was drying now but where before the ornate dagger had been buried deep into his chest, there was now just a dark crimson hole.

'And yet the door has been locked the whole time?' Boyle continued, leaning over, and reviewing the wound.

'Yes, I was the last person to leave the room and when I shut the door, the dagger was most certainly here,' Doctor Carson continued, utterly bewildered.

'Hmm, this is becoming a most peculiar crime,' Inspector Boyle said, scratching his nose as he reviewed the body.

'Somebody must have come and taken it...but why?!'

'That is the question, doctor! Could be the killer was fearful they had left fingerprints on the handle but until we find the weapon, we can only surmise their intentions,' Boyle began, once more reaching for his notebook.

'It certainly looks that way,' Doctor Carson replied, still shocked by the latest development.

'Was the house cold last night doctor when you were trying to sleep?'

'What an extraordinarily odd question!'

'Bear with me, doctor!' Boyle pleaded.

'Yes, as a matter of fact, the house was very chilly last night.'

'Peculiar then, is it not, that Mr Avery would be lying on top of the covers?'

Doctor Carson followed the gaze of the wily Inspector and was rather dumbfounded when he noticed such a seemingly unimportant fact such as that this would have caught the Inspector's eye. He feared perhaps Inspector Boyle was beginning to lose his marbles.

'I wouldn't have even paid it a single thought,' he replied.

'It's points like that, my dear doctor, which can make or break a peculiar case such as this,' Boyle replied as his attention moved to the floorboards beside and under the bed.

'I must say your methods are certainly unorthodox, Inspector.'

'Should there only be orthodox methods for an investigation? Should I have a magnify glass?' Inspector Boyle replied in his dry humorous way.

'Well no, I suppose not....' Doctor Carson blushed slightly.

'Don't fret, doctor – I am sure my methods may come across as unusual to you but, I assure you, they have helped me countless times during my career,' Boyle smiled as he got on to his hands and knees and peered under the bed.

'Oh, I'm sure they have! Even we doctors have our own ways of operating 'outside of the norm' from time to time!' Carson chimed in, grateful for the Inspector's easy-going nature.

Getting back to his feet and dusting down his trousers, Inspector Boyle pulled out his notebook once more and wrote a note whilst loudly exclaiming: 'Just as I suspected.'

'What is it?!'

'There are no slippers by the bed, or indeed under it.'

'Slippers?!'

'Yes, doctor. Were there slippers laid out by your bed?'

'Well, yes, as a matter of fact.'

'Exactly – it's common practice in the midst of winter, especially in a house as distinguished as this.'

'But I'm sorry, I don't see how missing slippers could possibly help us with this investigation.'

'It tells me that, perhaps, Mr Avery wasn't in the room when he was stabbed.'

'What?!' Doctor Carson spluttered.

'Part of my job, doctor, is to theorise. Sometimes, crimes can look entirely cut and dried and yet be anything but. Often, by moving the body, a killer is ensuring we do not find the original crime scene – making it impossible to collect vital clues.'

'It's extraordinary! But yet I can see the logic in that approach,' said Doctor Carson. He had heard of Boyle's unique ways of working but only now was he increasingly beginning to understand Lady Avery's perception of Inspector Boyle as an extremely competent man. If his theories proved true, he might even be quite exceptional.

'We must, therefore, accomplish two things moving forward, doctor.'

'Go on.'

'First, we must interview each person in this house and establish their movements since last night. And, secondly, we must try and find an alternative crime scene.'

'Well, I should say that will be a very hard task.'

'It very likely will be, but in my experience, doctor, things we want to hide have a tendency of coming to light in time.'

As they finalised their search of Gerald Avery's room, Doctor Carson found himself thinking once more: 'Yes, it would appear our Inspector Boyle could yet prove to be quite exceptional.'

Inspector Boyle's next move was to gather all the guests in the drawing room. He wanted to see everyone together to better understand the dynamics within the household. It was a method he had successfully utilised in the past and one he felt could determine if the killer was, in fact, likely to be one of the household.

As he and Doctor Carson walked in, they found the ensemble spread throughout the room. A sombre atmosphere met them as Inspector Boyle took the lead, introducing himself to the collective group.

Present, by the fireplace, was Lady Avery, dressed in black, and, sat next to her, Richard Haymer, the young man holding tightly onto his aunt's frail hand, comforting her. Mrs Langtry and her stepdaughter Lillie were sat in the window booth with Mr Mckelvie. The Colonel sat in an armchair to the right, whilst the household staff made up of Harley, Kumba, the young maid Amy and the driver, Conroy, all stood awkwardly on the far side of the room.

'Inspector, must we stay much longer? I really must be getting back down to Fowey,' Mrs Langtry bemoaned once the Inspector had finished his introduction.

Addressing the entire room he responded: 'Ladies and gentlemen, I am sorry to have to keep you here under such difficult and upsetting circumstances, but, due to the adverse weather, it is unlikely I can get additional constables up here in the coming couple of days. With this in mind, I must insist that everyone stays here at the property until I and the doctor have had the opportunity to interview each one of you.'

'Doctor! The extent of your skills seems to know no ends!' Haymer quipped.

Ignoring the younger man's statement, Inspector Boyle continued: 'It shouldn't take us more than a few hours and, once the process is completed, then there should be no reason for you to stay here any longer.'

This seemed to satisfy the reluctant group and with that the Inspector asked Mr Mckelvie if he would kindly join them in the library to obtain his statement first.

But before he could make his way to the door, the Colonel sprung from his seat and grabbed the Inspector's arm. 'I must insist that we speak first, Inspector,' he said in a low, urgent tone.

'If you insist, Colonel. Mr Mckelvie, we will call for you shortly.'

With that the three of them left the remaining

occupants and headed to the library.

CHAPTER FIFTEEN

Colonel Avery's statement

'Smoke, Colonel?' The Inspector asked, trying to ease his way into conversation with the elderly man, who seemed a little unnerved.

'No, thank you, Inspector – now listen here, I've seen him!'

'Seen who exactly, Colonel?'

'The murderer of course!'

'You mean to say you know who it is?!' Doctor Carson was stunned.

'You're not listening doctor, I didn't say I know who he is, just that I've seen him!' The older man seemed agitated at having to explain his wording.

'Please do explain your meaning, Colonel,' Inspector Boyle said in a matter-of-fact tone, although Carson noticed he was watching the Colonel's face intently.

'I was out on my morning walk. Clears the head, you know, a stroll in the fresh air.

'Yes, quite, and then?'

'I made my way down to the lake and that's when I saw him, over in the trees, lurking he was, but I spotted him,' he said proudly.

'And you don't know who it was? Could you make out any features?'

'Never seen the man before in my life, that's for sure. But he was a foreigner, no doubt about it!'

Doctor Carson couldn't help but feel sceptical about the Colonel's account. At a certain age, didn't everything bad that happened become the fault of someone 'foreign'? But if Inspector Boyle felt the same way, he certainly wasn't showing it outwardly.

'What made you sure he was foreign,' the Inspector asked calmly, noting everything down in meticulous and neat handwriting in his notebook.

'It's the skin! You always can tell. Olive colouring, but not the sort you'd get from a holiday!' He continued: 'I have spent many a year out in the colonies you know, Inspector, so I can tell a man who is native to warmer climates.'

'That's quite a useful skill, Colonel,' the Inspector said without a hint of irony.

Pleased with the young Inspector's manner, the Colonel nodded his head and continued.

'He was a short chap, plump too I'd say, but what I certainly saw was the olive skin and the jet-black hair – no doubt foreign.'

'If you had to hazard a guess, whereabouts would you say he is from.... using your unique experience as a well-travelled man,' the Inspector flattered his witness.

'I am not a man who likes to guess Inspector, but if I were to, I'd say he was Mediterranean or possibly North African.'

'Thank you, Colonel, you have been most helpful with this account,' he replied, noting in his notebook the description of the shady figure from the forest. 'Could you now let us know your movements last night, shall we say from 8pm onwards?'

'I suppose it's a formality! Well, I was playing cards at that time – the doctor here can testify to that.' He started pointing at Doctor Carson, who nodded his acknowledgement of the fact.

'We finished the game just after 10, everyone

was in good spirits, but Gerald had been rather tiresome, so I was keen to retire to my room rather than join in with a drink and smoke.'

'Tiresome, you say? Had he offended someone?'

'Oh, not in the traditional sense – he was talking about his plans for the Court, foolish boy! Never appreciated the birth right this name provided!' The colour in the old boy's face reddened as he spoke.

Inspector Boyle wrote more notes in his notebook but said nothing.

'Anyway, once the cards finished, I went straight to my room, bumping into Harley on route. I informed him I would need my walking boots ready for the morning as I intended to go for a stroll after breakfast. Then I got into bed and that's the job lot until I woke bright and early as I always do at 6.30.'

'You didn't hear anything in the night?' the doctor asked eagerly.

'Not a bean! I slept rather well as it happens,' he replied.

'Well, that's all for now Colonel – thank you for your insight and we will be sure to investigate the man you saw in the grounds,' Inspector Boyle stated, shaking hands with the elder man as he left the room.

Once the Colonel had made his retreat, leaving

the two men standing in the library, Doctor Carson turned to the Inspector and asked his opinion on the turn of events.

'Well, Inspector? What do you make of that? Surely an external party being involved throws a spanner in the works?!'

'It certainly adds another dimension to the case, doctor, I can't deny that.'

'We must surely focus our energies on locating this man?'

'No, I wouldn't say so, not yet anyway,' Boyle replied, the glint in his eye appearing once more. 'For now, we must continue our interviews with those present over the course of the weekend.'

'But what if this mysterious man is the murderer?! We can't let him slip the net!'

'Relax, dear doctor – in my long years dealing with gruesome crime, there is one thing I've learnt…'

'Yes?'

'Even the most heinous of crimes have a motive and that motive very often evolves around family issues.'

'So, you maintain the killer is, in fact, one of the guests here?'

'That I cannot say for certain…yet,' he replied cautiously, adding: 'but what I mean is, if there are answers to be found, including about our mysterious stranger, I would hazard a bet that those answers lie between these four walls.'

CHAPTER SIXTEEN

Lady Avery's defiance

The next guest the Inspector called for was the remaining head of the household, Lady Avery. He was keen to get her statement quickly, conscious of the terrible trauma she had endured so unexpectedly.

As she entered the library though, he was rather surprised to find not a frail old widow in the depths of mourning but a strong, determined woman who walked with a sense of purpose and confident steps which defied her years.

'Lady Avery, thank you for agreeing to give a statement at what I can only imagine is an extremely difficult and upsetting time,' he began diplomatically.

'Naturally, Inspector,' she replied formally as she sat down on the sofa alongside the fireplace, 'I am a pragmatic person and know the importance of you ascertaining the facts as quickly as possible.'

'Yes, it is, indeed, imperative we get as much detail as we can. Thank you, Lady Avery.'

'Well, ask away,' she waved her hand flamboyantly as if batting away an imaginary fly with her hand, eager to commence the interview.

'Perhaps we could begin by learning of your movements last night following the reading of your late husband's will?'

'I went to the drawing room with my sister-in-law, Mrs. Langtry, and Mr Mckelvie…this would have been around 8pm.'

'And you remained there for the evening?'

'Yes, the three of us had coffee in the window booth by the fire. It was snowing awfully outside and around 9.30pm I determined I would retire to my room. It had been a rather trying day.'

'Well, of course, all things considered,' Inspector Boyle replied, writing in his ever-present notebook. 'Did you remain in your room for the duration of the night?'

'What an odd question! Of course, I did! I sat and read for about 45 minutes before turning off my light and going to sleep. I didn't then wake until Harley knocked this morning.'

'And that's when you learnt the news of your son, Mr Avery?'

'That is correct Inspector,' she replied in a blunt tone.

'Thank you, Lady Avery, you have been most helpful! Just one more thing, do you remember hearing footsteps on the landing at any point?'

'Well, really Inspector, I find this line of questioning to be most bizarre.'

'I don't mean to trouble you, your ladyship!' he replied bowing his head, 'I just need to ensure we cover all the bases.'

'No, Inspector, once I retired to my room, I don't recall hearing anything until I was awoken to Harley knocking on my door, as I told you.'

'Thank you, Lady Avery that will be all.'

As she stood, her demeanour suggested she was less than pleased with the Inspector's line of questioning, but she smiled civilly in his direction before turning her attention to Doctor Carson.

'Doctor, I wonder whether you might be so kind as to call on me later once you have finished interviewing our guests of course!'

'Certainly, Lady Avery, I would be delighted.'

With that, she nodded her approval and walked defiantly from the room.

Inspector Boyle was certainly impressed with the woman he had just interviewed but her demeanour ensured he hadn't really gained any great level of insight into her personality. He fancied that had she not been of the fairer sex, she would have made quite a formidable Inspector herself.

CHAPTER SEVENTEEN

Mrs Langtry rambles on

Mrs Langtry was the next member of the party to make her way into the 'Inspector's Lair' as Haymer was jovially declaring it.

As she entered the room and took a seat at the Inspector's insistence, she fidgeted nervously. Inspector Boyle deduced immediately that she was a polar opposite of her sister-in-law. Where Lady Avery had been resolute, calm and composed, Mrs Langtry sat awkwardly in her chair, clasping her hands tightly in her lap as she glanced in an almost terrified way at the two men in front of her.

Inspector Boyle decided that for this particular

interview they would have to try a different tact and asked Doctor Carson to pour Mrs Langtry a cup of tea.

Once she was suitably served and altogether in a calmer disposition, the conversation began.

'Thank you, Mrs Langtry, for coming to see us.'

'Oh, it is all so dreadful,' she began, the cup in her hand wavering. 'I can't tell you how bad this has been for my nerves.'

'There, there, Mrs Langtry. I know you've had quite an ordeal and I assure you we will do everything we can to have the matter resolved in as timely a manner as possible.' The Inspector spoke in a reassuring tone.

'I do hope so, Inspector. I really do long to return to Fowey.'

'Yes, I know it well!' the Inspector replied. 'Beautiful coastal town.'

'Oh, it certainly is! One really must experience the fresh sea air and walk the coastline – it is such a splendid part of the world,' she mused, clearly brightening at the thought of her hometown.

'Your late husband was quite the artist, I believe?'

'How kind of you to note that, Inspector.' She beamed at the mention of her husband. 'Jeffery really was quite a talent you know! Such a shame he wasn't appreciated as well in life as he has been in death, but such is the artists' curse, I suppose!' she continued distantly, as if talking to herself.

'Indeed, it does seem artists are better appreciated in the afterlife. A tragic accident if I recall correctly?'

'Yes, it was truly heart-breaking. He left in the morning so full of life and vigour! Spending a day at sea painting the coastline from its most beautiful angle, as he put it. Then the storm hit, and he was gone forever,' her voice faded as she stared emptily into the fire.

Inspector Boyle suspected it was also the day her life, at least as she'd knew it, ended forever.

The room fell silent for just a moment and Doctor Carson felt as if both the other occupants were lost in their own little worlds. He coughed a grunt like cough, and it had the desired effect as Inspector Boyle returned to his usual line of enquiry.

'Right then, Mrs Langtry, I must ask you a couple of questions but please be assured this is just a formality.'

'OK, Inspector, I will do what I can to answer.'

'Excellent! Could you begin by telling me your movements last night?'

'Well, let's see…' she paused, frowning as she fell deep into thought.

'Ah, yes! Following the reading of my brother's will, I joined Lady Avery and that solicitor fellow, Mr Mckelvie, for coffee in the drawing room.'

'I see and how was the will reading? I imagine it is a tough thing to have to experience?'

Doctor Carson frowned at this question. It was the first time that Inspector Boyle had deviated from his usual script and certainly wasn't a question he had posed to either Colonel or Lady Avery.

'Yes, it was a tough experience. Oh, I did love my brother dearly,' she sighed. 'He was so kind to me and to Lillie, especially after Jeffery's passing.'

'He left you a generous pension I believe?'

'Oh,' she blushed. 'Yes, he was most generous to me and my brother. We have always been well cared for ever since he took over the estate following dear Papa's passing.'

'I'm glad to hear it. So, overall, you felt the will was fair and just to everyone?' Inspector Boyle probed.

'Well, I wouldn't like to say for other people, but certainly it seemed my brother had taken care of everyone. Why, even the servants had arrangements!' She looked rather flustered by this line of questioning by the Inspector, and Doctor Carson couldn't help but feel this was exactly what Boyle was hoping to achieve.

'Yes, a most generous man indeed,' Inspector Boyle smiled warmly, alleviating the tension from the room effortlessly. 'Well, we won't delay you much further, you have been most gracious with your time! But can you just tell me what time you retired for the evening, Mrs Langtry?'

'It would have been.... well, about 9.45pm I suspect! Lady Avery had gone to bed a few minutes previously and I recall talking with Mr Mckelvie about the importance of bees.'

'Bees?'

'Yes, bees! We were discussing how crucial they are to the survival of humanity.'

'I see... and you recall this conversation ending around 9.45pm?' Inspector Boyle asked, trying to get the conversation back on track.

'It was exactly 9.45pm Inspector. I recall Mr Mckelvie saying he felt a tad under the weather and was keen to get a good night's rest. Naturally, I couldn't blame him, I myself have felt the ill effects of this cold storm over the last couple of days,' she carried on.

'But the time Mrs Langtry?'

'Oh yes, of course. I know it was 9.45pm because

as Mr Mckelvie got up to leave, the small clock on the mantle chimed again as it had at 9.30pm when Lady Avery had gone to bed. I knew it must be a quarter to the hour.'

'Ah, I see, well that's most helpful, Mrs Langtry, most helpful. Do you have anything else to add doctor?'

Doctor Carson had been seldom more than a curious bystander during the interview, but he sensed the Inspector was hoping he would ask his now trademark question and dutifully obliged.

'Yes, I wonder, Mrs Langtry, if you heard anything during the course of the night? A disturbance perhaps or footsteps outside in the hall?'

'You mean did I hear the murderer making his retreat?' She shuddered at the thought. 'I heard nothing and shouldn't have wished to either!'

'Then that's everything!' Inspector Boyle said jovially, standing from his chair. 'Thank you so much for your assistance, Mrs Langtry.'

'Thank you, Inspector, I do hope this ordeal will soon be over.'

He bowed his head in acknowledgment and stood tentatively as she made her way from the room. Once she had left and the two were alone once more, he turned to the doctor and smirked.

'I suppose, doctor, you have some questions

around my choice of questioning?'

'Why, exactly right!' the doctor exclaimed, as if the Inspector had read his mind.

'It's simple really – I suspect Mrs Langtry will be quite forthcoming with the news of her questioning to anyone who cares to listen,' Boyle said.

'But how is that helpful?'

'Ah! There is nothing more helpful, doctor. I suspect the remainder of our group will now pre-plan their statements and, in doing so, any untruth is sure to show itself to us plainly.'

'Rather extraordinary!' Doctor Carson mused, impressed with the unorthodox approach.

'It might not help us and yet… it might just lead us onto the right track,' Boyle replied cryptically.

'What was the meaning behind asking her of her late husband's death, Inspector? Surely that was rather rotten in the circumstances – stirring up the past like that?'

'It was, I assure you, a necessary line of enquiry,'

'How so?'

'Just a little theory of mine, but, for now, I shall keep that one a closely guarded secret of my own.'

The glint was back in his eyes.

CHAPTER EIGHTEEN

Richard Haymer loses his cool

Richard Haymer came into the room with a spring in his step, certainly not in the least bit concerned by the idea of having his statement taken by the police.
Shaking hands warmly with Inspector Boyle, he sat in a leather wingback chair by the window and placed one leg casually over the other, pulling his cigarettes from his pocket.

'Smoke, Inspector?'

'Thank you, Mr Haymer, most kind,' the other man indulged his latest visitor, reaching out and taking a cigarette and match.

'Our good doctor here doesn't smoke, so I hope he doesn't mind if we do?' Haymer said charmingly.

'Oh no, please don't stop on my account!'

'Jolly good! So, I suppose you'll be wanting to know all about my whereabouts and whether I saw a murderer stalking the grounds?!'

'Did you also see the shadowy figure in the grounds?' the doctor exclaimed before thinking.

'Shadowy figure?!' Haymer's face was suddenly awash with confusion, suggesting he was utterly unaware of such things.

'Oh, I….' Doctor Carson blushed brightly; conscious his over eagerness had put his foot in it.

'Relax, dear doctor,' Inspector Boyle smiled warmly. 'It is good to clarify these matters.'

Haymer's confusion continued: 'Care to fill me in chaps? I feel a bit out of the loop here!'

'Sorry, Mr Haymer! The shadowy figure the doctor mentions was witnessed by the Colonel out by the lake early this morning, just shortly after the body of Mr Avery had been discovered.'

'Well, I say! Surely, that's our man then?' Haymer stated in a shocked tone.

'We are investigating all leads,' Boyle replied professionally. 'Can we say then that you didn't see the man?'

'I haven't seen anyone at all on the grounds, Inspector, that's the truth of it. Damn wish I had though, rotten scoundrel! Did the Colonel get a good look at his face?'

'He has given us a description, yes.'

'Well? Are you able to disclose that information, Inspector? I'd like to know what I need to be conscious of in case he returns!'

'I suppose there's no harm in it! Let's see here,' Inspector Boyle skimmed through his notebook and found his notes from his previous meeting with the Colonel.

'Ah, yes here we are – the man is said to have been foreign, of a dark complexion, with jet black hair and a rather short height.'

Doctor Carson couldn't help but notice the reaction the description had on Haymer. His face seemed to pale instantly, a look of shock in his eyes as if he had registered something that didn't sit well will him. Carson looked quickly over to the Inspector, whose mouth seemed to show just the slightest signs of a smile as he wrote quickly in his notebook before asking in a casual tone: 'Not too much to go on but there we have it! Least you can be wary now, eh Mr Haymer?'

'Eh? Oh, oh yes!' the young man stuttered, the confidence of his manner evading him as he struggled to regather his composure.

'Well then, with that settled – what say we get

down to it? Can you tell us in your own words your movements last night?'

'Last night? Oh yes, quite,' Haymer said, a smile returning to his face as the colour was restored to his complexion. Whatever had caused his startled reaction was being quickly suppressed.

'Following dinner, I joined Gerald, Colonel Avery, Miss Morris and the good doctor here in a few games of cards in the Library.'

'And I note from the doctor that you all finished around 10?'

'Yes, I believe that's correct, Doctor Carson and the Colonel retired for the night, whilst I remained with Miss Morris for a few minutes discussing my travels in Africa.'

'Did you both then go to bed?'

'Well, I can hardly speak for Miss Morris, but I believe she said she was going to go and check on her stepmother. Mrs Langtry had been suffering with a cold.'

'I see, and did you go straight to your room?'

'I did not, as it happens. It had been quite a busy day and I was certainly not ready to unwind. So, I had a cigarette and sat here reading a book,' he motioned at the variety of choices available on the shelves surrounding them.

Inspector Boyle made a note in his notebook and

continued: 'What time did you go to bed, Mr Haymer, and did you awaken at all during the course of the night?'

'Let's see, I went to bed around 11.30pm. I remember the house was eerily quiet and I was grateful to get to my room. This old place gives me the chills! But once asleep sometime soon after that, I slept like a baby until the morning.'

'Very good, Mr Haymer. One last thing – were you pleased with the outcome of your uncle's will?'

'What an extraordinary question!' It wasn't the first time the Inspector had been met with such an answer that evening.

'I only ask, sir, because you were the eldest son of the eldest born. It would be natural for you to have inherited this estate and the wealth that comes with it on your uncle's passing and, yet it went to your cousin.'

Richard Haymer looked unsettled once more, although this time his face wasn't so much pale as slowly crimsoning with anger.

'Inspector, if you are insinuating in any way that I may have begrudged my cousin inheriting Oakford Court, and that, in a mad fit of rage, I proceeded to kill him, I can categorically assure you you're utterly wasting your time, barking up the wrong tree!'

'Mr Haymer, sir, I assure you my intention wasn't to insult you or to insinuate any such thing,' Boyle replied calmly. 'I simply must establish the facts and as the will reading presents a plausible reason for motive, I must, as a matter of course, ask such questions.'

Haymer eyed the Inspector sternly and then the doctor, his mind seemed to be awash with deep thought as if he were weighing up his next move. Then, he gave a big sigh, and the anger began to subside.

'Yes, of course, I suppose you must, Inspector. It's just the most rotten of thoughts to think I would, or even could, be involved in such a horrible crime! But, to answer your question, I was pleased with the will. I've never held any desire to be tied down to the responsibilities of my family name and the only good that could have come of my late father's passing is the fact that such a burden passed to his younger brother, my uncle, and then on through his bloodline and not mine.'

'I see, thank you, sir, for answering the question and please forgive the need to ask you.'

'Of course, Inspector. I, too, must apologies for my rash tone, it has been a trying time being back here at Oakford Court.'

Inspector Boyle nodded his understanding and stood to shake hands with Mr Haymer, who made his retreat to the door far less breezily than he had made his entrance.

'I am awfully sorry, Inspector' Doctor Carson blurted out. 'I have been an utter fool.'

'What on earth are you on about, doctor?'

'I blurted out about the shadowy figure, without even thinking that you might want to keep that under wraps.'

The Inspector chuckled heartily to himself as he slapped the doctor affectionately on the shoulder.

'Doctor, whether you realise it or not – you're making quite the detective.'

'There's no need to mollycoddle me, Inspector, I certainly do not want to undermine this investigation,' Carson added, and hung his head, embarrassed.

'Undermine? Why, my dear boy, you may very well have cracked our first proper lead!'

'You can't be serious!' Doctor Carson exclaimed.

'Oh, I am quite serious!' Boyle replied, a satisfied smirk spreading across his face. 'Tell me, doctor, did you notice anything odd when we shared the Colonel's description of the mysterious man?'

Doctor Carson frowned. He wasn't sure what the Inspector was getting at. He had hardly noticed anything untoward, and yet, thinking back, there WAS something that seemed a little out of place in the way Haymer had reacted.

'Come to think of it, Inspector, I hardly paid any attention at the time - too wrapped up in my own blunder! But Richard Haymer certainly seemed… well, flustered at the description.'

'Spot on, doctor!' Inspector Boyle beamed at his young protégé in the making. 'We'll make a detective of you yet!'

'But what does it all mean?!'

'What it means, my boy, is that Mr Haymer just might have recognised someone he knows from that description, and, if I were to hazard an educated guess, not someone he wants to see again in a hurry.'

'Well, I'll be! That is quite an interesting theory, Inspector! Does this mean Mr Haymer could quite possibly be involved in the murder of his uncle? And, that this mystery man is his accomplice?'

'At this time, I cannot rule it out.'

Doctor Carson shuddered at the thought. 'He is such a charming young man, surely a cold-blooded killer cannot be so amiable?'

'From my experience, doctor, even the most charming of men can be driven to murder.'

CHAPTER NINETEEN

A box to be ticked in Windsor

The old butler moved into the room with the airy, silent movement of one so well versed to a life of service. So quietly did he move through the room that Inspector Boyle wondered if he knew the exact location of every creaky floorboard in the old building.

It was a thought that both amused and intrigued the Inspector in equal measure. As he acknowledged the butler and asked him to take a seat, he quickly made a note of the point in his notebook.

'Thank you for taking the time to meet with us, Harley,' he began as usual.

'I am at your service, Inspector,' the old man

bowed his head courteously.

'Now, as I'm sure you're aware, we are trying to ascertain the movements of each of the occupants during the night. I will be talking to the other servants when I can, but it would be greatly appreciated if you can tell us their normal routines of an evening, so we can save some time?'

'Of course, sir. When her ladyship retires for the evening, Kumba would usually prepare her hot cocoa and take it up to her room. Once her ladyship is settled, she then is free to retire herself ready for the morning cleaning prior to Lady Avery rising for breakfast.'

'Very good,' Boyle made some short, scribbled notes in his book.

'Conroy the chauffeur would not be needed of a usual evening, especially in weather such as this, and would most likely be found in the kitchen where chef provides a warm late snack. Earlier in the evening, he would likely be cleaning the car and taking care of maintenance jobs, being something of a handyman.'

'The young maid who found Mr Avery's body?'

'Yes, Amy Sheldon, the newest member of the staff, having only joined us a few months ago. She was given the night off last night, having worked additional hours to help Kumba following Lord

Avery's passing.'

'I see. And Miss Sheldon came to Oakford with good references?'

'Oh, decidedly so, sir. I personally review all staff references and hers came from a most acceptable background. The Hall-Say's near Windsor, no less.'

Inspector Boyle was familiar with the Hall-Say's and noted the connection in his notebook.

'Very well, thank you, Harley. Now, please tell us of your whereabouts.'

'Certainly, sir. I always ensure the guests are settled for the night before retiring myself. The majority of the younger guests where in the library playing cards with Colonel Avery. Lady Avery, Mr Mckelvie and Mrs Langford were in the drawing room having tea. Once the three of them retired, I ensured the drawing room was in order and replenished the drinks for the group in the library. Once everyone had retired, I ensured the remaining lights were turned off for the night, locked the main doors and made my way to my quarters.'

'And what time did you turn in?'

'I would say it was nearly midnight by the time I eventually got to my room.'

'Who was the last to go up other than yourself?'

'That would have been Mr Haymer, sir. I remember it was close to 11.30pm by the time he had finished reading in the library.'

'I see, and did he go straight from there to his room?'

'I believe he did, sir, he was just about to ascend the stairs when I saw him, and he wished me goodnight. I then proceeded to make my way to the library and ensured the lights were turned out and all was as it should be following the card game.'

'So, you didn't actually see Mr Haymer go up to his room?'

'Well no, sir, but then other than the Colonel and Mr Mckelvie, I didn't see anyone go specifically to their room.'

'Quite so. I mean to say that you didn't know for certain if Mr Haymer had continued to go upstairs? He may, for example, have remained on the ground floor?'

Harley showed the slightest expression of doubt, his aged face scrunching as he thought through the possibility.

'I suppose that's possible, sir, but I cannot see a reason for him doing so?'

'Not to worry, Harley, it was just to ensure we have covered all angles,' Boyle reassured the elderly man, all the while making notes in his notebook.

Doctor Carson cleared his throat 'Harley could you tell us where in the house you were when the body was discovered the next morning?'

Inspector Boyle approved of the question with a sly smile.

'I was downstairs in the breakfast pantry, doctor. I had just seen the Colonel leave the house for his morning walk. He wouldn't miss it regardless of the weather. Then I heard the commotion from upstairs and came as quickly as I could.'

'Well, I think that's all we will need for now, Harley, thank you. I think we would like to talk to each of the household staff at the earliest possible convenience, but we will endeavour to do so around their workloads.'

Harley bowed his head. 'Thank you, sir, I will ensure each is readily at your disposal.'

With that he made his exit as silently as he had appeared, softly closing the door with a deft hand.

Doctor Carson turned to Inspector Boyle and waited eagerly for any sign that the interview had provided something illuminating. For his own part, it clarified one key point; Haymer wasn't actually seen upstairs, meaning he could have slipped back down and met an accomplice.

'Well, doctor, I think our work is done here for the time being,' Boyle began.

'Yes? Surely Harley's testimony proves Haymer had the opportunity to be left alone downstairs?'

'Perhaps. But perhaps not. Either way, it isn't a point I would get too hung up on right now.'

Doctor Carson was flabbergasted by the Inspector's dismissal of the point he felt was most significant.

'You cannot surely believe there is a point more significant?!'

'Oh, but there are plenty, doctor. This point is, I agree, a significant one, but perhaps that is because we WANT it to be so?'

'I do see your logic, Inspector, but you have to see the means of opportunity are there for Haymer?'

'Perhaps they are, but one could suggest the same opportunities were present for Harley himself? Perhaps even clearer opportunities, as by his own admission, he was the last to retire for the evening.'

'I, I hadn't thought of it like that but, by jove, you have a point! This really is most frustrating! Every time we seem to find a piece of the puzzle, another creates itself.'

'Don't be dispirited, doctor! The key to any case is to separate the important from the unimportant. We have now clear lines of enquiry which we must explore further.'

Inspector Boyle rose from his chair and encouraged the doctor to follow suit.

'Where are we going?'

'I think we ought to go down to the lake and check for any clues following the Colonel's statement. But, first, I must make a telephone call to Windsor.'

'Windsor?'

'Amy Sheldon's former employer, the Hall-Say's. I intend to ascertain my own reference to '*tick that box*' so to say!'

Not for the first time, Doctor Carson was thoroughly perplexed.

'You can't suspect the maid is the killer, surely?'

'Truthfully, I do not believe this to be so, but it is a line of enquiry and considering that Miss Sheldon is the only noticeable change in the staff in the last couple of years, it is one we need to address.'

'I see the logic, Inspector. Well, you make the call and I'll ask Harley if there are some walking boots we can borrow. It's still rather ghastly out there.'

They both nodded in agreement and went their separate ways. The Inspector headed directly for the ground floor lobby to make his phone call to the Berkshire police force and Doctor Carson headed off to find the elderly butler once more.

CHAPTER TWENTY

The lake hides a clue

Once the Inspector had finished his call to the Berkshire police, who had promised to check Amy Sheldon's references as soon as possible, he made his way to the boot room where he found Doctor Carson attempting to squeeze his feet into a pair of wellington boots which seemed a size or more too small.

'Everything OK there, doctor?'

'I seem to be having a slight issue with these boots! Every size under the sun in here except mine!'

'Rather unfortunate!' Boyle chuckled.

'It's just typical! I asked Harley about it and he

said there is usually every size lined up neatly across this back wall.' Carson waved his hand along the wall behind him, where immaculately clean dark green boots were neatly lined-up from smallest to largest in size.

Inspector Boyle's tone immediately changed, a serious look adorning his face as he pulled his notebook from his jacket breast pocket for the umpteenth time that day.

'Harley says there is normally a pair in every size?'

'Well, yes…. why is that a concern?

'Don't you see, doctor? A pair is missing. It implies someone has used them; don't you think?! Did Harley say when the pair were noticed missing?'

'No, as far as I could tell he was noticing it at the same time as I was. Neither of us paid particular attention to it, boots will be used this time of year, after all.'

Boyle nodded in agreement, but his eyes lit up brightly as he scribbled another note in his book.

'What size were the boots you needed, doctor?'

'Size 9 as it happens.'

'Well, there is some good news…'

'Yes?' Carson raised his head from his boot struggles with a sign of optimism.

'I am a size 7 and they have the perfect pair,' Boyle quipped, much to the frustration of his companion.

Once they both had their boots on and had wrapped up sufficiently against the cold in large overcoats, they opened the large front door and made their way round the side of the Court to the back patio.

The snow was melting as the milder temperatures set in, but with a brisk biting wind it still felt every bit the middle of winter as they navigated the icy pathway across the terrace and down onto the hardened grass.

The grounds had long been a beautiful setting at the Court with an ornate, stone fountain shaped like a mythical dolphin sitting centrally to the lawn. It was surrounded in summer by a beautiful circular rose garden that currently looked forlorn in the harsh winter frost.

As they passed the fountain, Doctor Carson was struck by the sight of the long, frozen icicles protruding down from the dolphin's mouth, frozen in time.

Past the fountain lay a small gravel path which led in a semi-circular loop to the foot of the man-made lake spreading widely across the landscape and surrounded on either side by heavy forestry which lined the estate's perimeter.

As the two men made their way onto the path, Doctor Carson asked the Inspector a question that had played on his mind ever since the murder had taken place.

'Inspector, in your expert opinion, is this a premeditated crime? It seems to me as if it were a crime of rage, one perhaps inspired by the revelations of the will – and, yet nobody seemingly lost out at its reading.'

'It is a good question, doctor and one I myself have been contending with since I arrived. The obvious answer is how you say it, and this could explain the knife being removed from the body. Yet, something about this crime just doesn't add up! How, for example, did our killer gain entry to the room of Gerald Avery?'

'I assumed the door was never locked. Or the killer had access with another key?' Carson noted his previous conversation with Mckelvie.

'Assumption, doctor, is something we in our profession cannot afford to entertain. Hard facts alone convict murderers. Plenty a bad person has escaped scot-free on circumstantial evidence.'

'Then, what are the facts?'

'Well, currently as we know them, Gerald

Avery's killer had access to the room, where he took the opportunity to kill Avery with a sharp ornate dagger that is now missing,' Boyle began, reciting the points from memory. 'We have a witness placing a mystery figure out here by the lake just hours later, who as of yet is unaccounted for, and, thus, we must assume has a role to play in the events which have taken place.'

'Yes, it's all clear when structured like that,' Doctor Carson agreed.

'And yet, clarity is the one thing we greatly lack!'

Their conversation had brought them to the edge of the lake where a small wooden bench was inscribed with the insignia of the Oakford dynasty. Boyle carefully noted the scene around him and the bench before walking to the water's edge.

'Remind me, doctor, where the Colonel stated he was standing?'

'It was about 5 feet to your right, away from the benches.'

Boyle nodded and carefully stepped out the paces in that direction. Arriving at the correct spot, he pointed out to the distant forest on the far-right side of the lake.

'There, doctor, I need you to stand here exactly where I stand now and point there.'

Doctor Carson joined him at the lakeside and aligned his arm to the Inspector's pointed location.

'Now what?'

'Now, I will walk around into the woods and emerge from the trees at the point you are indicating.'

'I see, and the point of this exercise, so I am clear?'

'The point is twofold; on the one hand, we need to find the exact area the mystery figure was seen. This could lead us to vital clues, and I am best placed to notice them without tampering with the scene. On the other, we need you to relive the Colonel's point of view; how clearly can you make out the figure you see emerging and how long does it take them to escape from view?'

'A sort of re-enactment after the fact?'

'Exactly that, my dear boy! Now stay still, I will be as quick as I can.'

With that, the Inspector marched off at pace around the side of the lake and disappeared into the forest. After a few moments, his figure was completely submerged by the threadbare wooden fortress of branches.

Doctor Carson felt his arm begin to ache and feared he might not be able to maintain the position required. A full minute passed, and his arm began to wobble ever so slightly, when he first saw the figure beginning to emerge from the darkness of the forest.

As Boyle made his way to the exact point Carson was signalling, he waved, allowing the doctor to mercifully rest his tired limb as he did his best to make out as much detail about the Inspector's figure as he could.

Another minute passed before he heard a feint call from the Inspector, muffled by the wind dancing across the frozen surface of the lake. Straining his eyes, he could just make out the waving hand of Boyle and realised his call was for Carson to join him around by the forest.

Dutifully, he began his trudge along the lake's perimeter slowly as he closed in on the Inspector's location. With each step, the blurred blob that was the Inspector became clearer and clearer. When Carson was less than a few feet away from the Inspector, he realised he was holding a large log in his hands.

'I say, had time to collect some firewood, did you?' he quipped.

'When did you first see me holding this log,' Boyle replied, with an intensity that suggested he meant business.

'Well, just as I arrived here and said it.'

'Aha! So, you can confirm you didn't notice it at any time before?'

'No, I certainly did not!' Carson replied, before adding with a frown: 'When did you have time to pick it up? I scarcely looked away from you for a moment during the walk here.'

'My dear doctor, I've had it the entire time.'

'You've what?!'

'I picked it up on my way through the forest and had it in my hand the entire time I've been stood here! All a little experiment of mine.'

'What's the meaning of it though?'

'I wanted to ascertain whether our mysterious figure may have been down here by the lake for a reason and whether the Colonel would have been able to see if he had anything on him at the time.'

'That's quite an excellent idea, Inspector! Most impressive.'

'Thank you, doctor. It was a little theory that I'm glad to say has paid off.'

'And what exactly do you suppose he was holding? The murder weapon?'

'Exactly, doctor, exactly!'

'Well, that is an intriguing proposition! But why?!'

'I am hoping the answer lies behind us...' Boyle replied with a smile on his face.

Carson turned and found himself facing the frozen lake.

'You think it's in there?!'

'Not in, on! See that patch of reeds over there,' Boyle pointed to a patch of semi-submerged reed stalks, poking defiantly through the frozen lake's surface.

'Why, yes!'

'I would hazard a guess our missing murder weapon is hidden concealed in those reeds.'

'An extraordinary theory, Inspector! Surely, it is too exposed out here. Why risk it?!'

'If I am right, doctor, I would theorise that our killer was eager to remove the weapon from the scene of the crime in a hurry. The weather has been awful out here and nobody in their right mind would venture out for too long. Suppose he bought it out here, flung it into the reeds and expected that by the time anyone came to pay the area too much attention, the ice would have melted and our weapon had found itself an ideal hiding spot at the bottom of a murky lake – almost impossible for us to locate.'

'Amazing! Truly amazing! It is an ingenious plan.'

'Yes, quite so. We must get out to those reeds and see if all is as I expect.'

'But how do you propose we do that?'

'That will be the problem! It must be nigh on 50 feet out to those reeds. We could walk it, but I wouldn't want to risk the ice cracking.'

'What about a boat? There must be one on the grounds.'

'It would be difficult to navigate the frozen surface but, yes, I see no alternative.'

The two men stood for a moment in silence, both pondering their options.

'Wait, pass me that log,' Carson uttered, taking the thick piece of wood from the Inspector.

Without delay, he turned and thrust the hard piece of wood down with a mighty force onto the icy surface. A groan and small chips met its impact, but the ice stood firm.

'I hope, doctor, you are not thinking what I suspect you're thinking?'

'It seems solid enough and the distance really isn't that far if I run.'

'It's ludicrous man! That ice could be sheet thin once you're out there, and if you fall in the water that's another death for me to contend with! I cannot allow it!'

'The simple fact, Inspector, is we do not have time to delay. This could be the missing piece of this puzzle and I, for one, cannot risk us losing it.'

Before the Inspector could object further, Carson exhaled heavily and made a run for the icy surface.

'Doctor!' Boyle remonstrated to no avail.

As Carson began his pacey movement across the surface, he soon struggled to maintain his grip. Mercifully, the soles of his boots gave him enough traction to remain upstanding and he continued as quickly as he could without slipping, the ice beginning to strain under his weight. More than once did he truly believe the ice was going to give way and he cursed himself for his spontaneity.

As he got closer and closer to the reeds, his heart began to beat faster as the realisation he was going to make it became overpowering. Then, disappointment took its place. There appeared to be nothing of note to see. He had expected a blood covered dagger to be sitting on the ice in the midst of the reeds, laying pristinely on the frozen surface covered in fingerprints. The missing piece.

'I can't see anything,' he called out dejectedly to the Inspector on the lakeside.

'You're sure? Some of those reeds are quite thick.'

Carson brushed through the stiff, frozen reeds, eagerly checking and hoping to find the dagger. But after another minute, he had checked all the reeds and it was apparent that nothing was lurking out on the ice.

Downcast, he cursed their misfortune and began to edge his way back to the bank. The creaking ice beneath his feet groaned as he once more covered its long, undisturbed surface. Inspector Boyle's face was etched with concern as he watched on in the distance.

One firm stride at a time, Carson was making progress across the lake's slippery surface and was less than 10 feet from the shoreline when his worst fear took hold. The ice beneath him began to crack.

'Run, doctor,' Inspector Boyle yelled, the second he heard the ice breaking.

Doctor Carson didn't need any prompting, pushing on as quickly as he could, the ice splitting below him, following him in a dangerous trail. Just a foot from the shoreline, the ice finally gave way, and he felt his foot begin to plunge through into the freezing water below. He feared his number was up and again cursed his luck at having come so close, all to no avail.

Then he felt a firm grip on his arm and found himself being hoisted onto the bank of the lake, landing hard on his side on the rock hard, frozen ground, the air stripped from his lungs.

'That was too close,' Boyle panted, laying on his back on the ground alongside the doctor.

'You... you saved me,' Carson managed to wheeze in reply.

'It's just damn lucky you didn't go through the ice!'

'All that and the dagger wasn't even there.'

'I know and had we lost you, doctor, it would have been for nothing! You cannot take such a foolish risk again; do you understand that?' The Inspector spoke in a fatherly tone, berating the younger man.

'You're right, Inspector, it was utter stupidity. I don't know what came over me.'

Boyle's tone softened. Despite his annoyance at the doctor's actions, he couldn't fault the younger man's determination to help solve this crime.

'You're determined to right wrongs, dear doctor! It's why you became a medical man and why you'd make a great detective! But nothing is worth sacrificing yourself for! It is frustrating, yes, that the weapon wasn't on the lake, but it's another line of enquiry we can now eliminate.

The more we eliminate, the closer we get to the truth.'

'Yes, you're quite right, Inspector! That is a healthy way to approach a setback.'

'In this line of work, doctor, setbacks are commonplace. It would be ill-advised to solve a murder without setback, it would leave one with too many questions and theories unresolved.'

They both lay on the hard, cold ground laughing a moment longer as they stared up at the bleak white sky high above.

'What now, Inspector?'

'We check the forest thoroughly for clues and then we head back to the house and interview the maid.'

Carson nodded and sat up, feeling a dull ache in his side as he did so. Getting to his feet, he helped Boyle up and the two men brushed themselves down.

'What sort of clues are we looking for?'

'Another little theory of mine, doctor, relates to those missing wellington boots. Had the killer used them to come out here and meet with our mysterious stranger, then we should see boot prints somewhere or, at the very least, prints which might help narrow down our search for the stranger himself.'

As they made their way through the forest, each man firmly keeping his eyes fixated on the frozen ground below, they hoped in vain for a bit of luck, anything to vindicate their efforts with physical evidence.

Suddenly, Doctor Carson gasped as his eyes honed in on a clearly made boot print, frozen in time on the hard ground just beneath him.

'Inspector! Over here!'

'What is it, doctor?'

'I think I've found a boot print,' the excitement in his voice was palpable.

Boyle hurried over and calmly lent down to examine the print in earnest for a good minute or so without saying another word. Doctor Carson's heart began to sink once more as he feared his eagerness to find a genuine clue could have led them simply to one of their own footprints! This panic was only momentary, though, as Boyle got back to his feet and warmly patted the doctor on the shoulder.

'I said we'd make a detective out of you, dear boy!'

'So, it is a clue Inspector?!'

'Oh, it certainly is – look closely, doctor, the print design mirrors that of our boots exactly.'

Leaning in, Carson could see the pattern emerging before his eyes and comparing it to his own awkwardly lifted foot, he could clearly see the same pattern.

'By George, it's an exact match!'

'This means my theory about the boots is correct and someone in the house must have taken a pair to come out here and inspect the location where the stranger was witnessed.'

'If that's so, Inspector, why risk it?'

'A valid point, indeed, but I suspect our man either intended to meet his partner out here or there was something left out here, a message perhaps. It would explain how they could stay in touch on developments within the house without the stranger being caught too close to the property itself.'

'It just all seems too messy for me, but you're the expert,' Carson stated, a look of utter confusion plastered across his face.

'Hmm "expert" is a loose term, doctor. You yourself are an expert of in your profession, yet I suspect you would readily accept you do not know everything there is to know about the human anatomy and the ills that can plague it?'

'Well, no, I shouldn't think I or, indeed, even the finest medical minds in the world know everything about such a complex thing.'

'Exactly! A murder crime is no different. Yes,

there are patterns, obvious reasonings and deductions, yet there is no one answer. Nor is there a guaranteed way to be an expert. I can merely use my experience to my advantage, just as a good doctor would do in treating a patient. Experience tells us we are on the right track, but we can never truly know the outcome until the very last moment.'

Carson nodded. The Inspector was a man wise beyond his years in many ways and, yet something in his manner suggested his cautious optimism was more than a simple façade. He sensed it was more based on fact. Carson suspected the Inspector already had a much clearer idea about what had happened at Oakford Court than he was willing to divulge just yet.

CHAPTER TWENTY ONE

Mr Mckelvie remembers

Doctor Carson was starting to feel exhausted. The interviews with the household had been going on sporadically for the last two hours now and his head was awash with possibilities regarding the murder of young Gerald Avery.

Inspector Boyle assured him they were making progress and that their time had been best utilised talking to the guests, something Doctor Carson was less sure of. He felt that if there was a mysterious stranger out by the lake, then why hadn't their efforts been focused outside, looking for clues that would lead to this man who, he felt in all logic, was almost certainly the killer?

It was a thought that continued to trouble him as Inspector Boyle re-entered the room with his next interviewee, Mr Mckelvie.

'How do you do, doctor,' Mckelvie smiled as he saw his friend sat pondering by the window.

'I only wish I knew, Mr Mckelvie!'

Joining the doctor at the window side table, Mr Mckelvie and the Inspector took their seats, and a fresh cup of coffee was poured by the latter for each of them. This was to be a much more informal conversation than the previous one.

'Mr Mckelvie, I have been told by Doctor Carson that you are very much like us, an outsider to what seems to be a decidedly personal family tragedy,' Inspector Boyle began.

'I must say, Inspector, it has been a most bizarre weekend thus far. I have known Lord and Lady Avery for some years – his Lordship was one of my very first clients when I joined the firm, but always remained only a professional acquaintance.'

'Yes, quite so. Can I begin by asking you about Lord Avery's last will and testament?'

'Of course, please ask away.'

'Firstly, from your experience was this in any way an unusual will?'

'No, Lord Avery's requests and legacies were no

different to many of my other wealthier clients. He was a man with a great sense of tradition and seemed intent on ensuring his family estate maintained just that.'

'I believe his relationship with his son was, at times, strained by Gerald's less than enthusiastic approach to his future responsibilities to this estate – is that something you were aware of?'

'Well, to a degree, I suppose I was. A couple of years ago, Lord Avery called upon my office quite incensed, determined to amend his will.'

'And did he disclose what had caused this outburst?'

'He wouldn't go into much detail but he did say he had reason to believe his son wasn't prepared to take his family commitment seriously and, as such, he may have no choice but to review the recipient of his legacy.'

'That seems quite a bold move for a traditionalist like Lord Avery?!'

'Yes, it was rather! I advised him to reconsider it at some length, as changing the will wasn't a straightforward procedure. I suggested he take the evening and we would reconvene the following day.'

'And he agreed?'

'Oh yes – and he had a much-changed outlook the next day. He said he had spent some time in the library considering his options and was now, on reflection, confident that the will was sufficient in its current form bar one minor change.'

'And, what was that change, Mr Mckelvie?'

'It was rather extraordinary in its simplicity. He wanted to change the wording, *'For my son Gerald'* to *'For my first-born son'* in the section discussing the estate.'

'Well, that does seem a rather bizarre thing to do doesn't it?' Doctor Carson interjected.

'Well yes... I suppose. Although I should point out that such changes aren't unheard of! Why, when I first started my career, I had a client who insisted I change the wording of his will to better reflect the social status of his soon-to-be married daughter.'

'Quite so. Well did Lord Avery give a reason for choosing to make this amend?' Boyle said, keen to get the conversation back on track as he sat poised to write Mckelvie's response in his notebook.

'He simply said he was keen to maintain wording which better suited the family's legacy and that would enable the estate to remain in the first-born bloodline.'

'I see, well that's clear enough, I suppose. Thank you, Mr Mckelvie. Coming back to the last 24 hours, has anything struck you as out of the ordinary?'

'You mean except the fact that the dagger used to kill Gerald Avery is missing?! I was gobsmacked when the doctor informed me of the findings of your visit to the crime scene.'

Doctor Carson blushed once more, suspecting he had said too much in his excitement at the preceding events and hoped the Inspector wouldn't be annoyed at his decision to bring Mckelvie into his confidence. It was, after all, he and Mckelvie who had begun the investigation of sorts.

Inspector Boyle didn't seem phased by the comment, simply giving the doctor a considered look before continuing: 'Well, naturally, that is a peculiar event, but I trust you didn't hear anything during the night?'

'Oh no, I was sound asleep until the commotion in the morning with the maid. I jumped out of bed and upon learning of her panic, rushed to the doctor's room'

'I see. We have learned from Colonel Avery that there could be a third party involved from outside of the house – he spotted someone out by the lake. Have you seen anyone at all?'

'I certainly haven't! But that is most interesting and surely proves the killer may not be within the household?!'

'Well, it could prove that, or it could be that our strange figure is working with someone from within the party. Either way, we will find out in due course, I'm confident of that!' Inspector Boyle replied cocksure of his investigation capabilities. 'So, you haven't seen a stranger, short, plump, with dark hair, likely foreign? I'm sorry to ask Mr...'

Boyle stopped in his tracks. As he had begun listing the description of the figure outlined by the Colonel, he saw the same look in Mr Mckelvie's face that he had seen earlier in Richard Haymer's, one of recognition.

'I, I think I know the man you're looking for Inspector.'

'Well, that is a turn-up for the books! Who is it, Mr Mckelvie?'

'I travelled down on the train from London with a man who meets that description.'

Doctor Carson's face lit up. 'You mean to say that Mr Pezzola matches the description of our stranger?!'

'Mr Pez...who?' Inspector Boyle, for perhaps the first time, was the one out of the loop.

'Mr Pezzola. He is an Italian salesman I met on the train down to Oakford. We got talking and it transpired he was coming to Oakford on a matter of business with an old acquaintance from the continent.'

'I see, and this acquaintance? You know who it is?'

'Oh yes, Inspector, you see he mentioned having met Mr Haymer during his time on the continent and said he was hoping to reconnect with him about some unresolved business transaction whilst on his way down to Cornwall.'

'Mr Haymer, eh? That is interesting! Did he say what the unresolved business might be?'

'Well, no, and I didn't really pry. I must confess I was hoping for a quiet journey, so while he made idle chat with me, I hardly placed any significance to it at all. That is until I spoke to the doctor about the conversation and he planted the idea that the timing was more than just a coincidence.'

'I quite agree with the doctor's assertion – I knew you had the making of a good detective, Doctor Carson!' Inspector Boyle beamed, the gleam back in his eyes. 'Well, if there is a connection, then Mr Haymer could be involved in the murder of his cousin?!' Doctor Carson, however, remained unconvinced of this theory, he just seemed too nice to be capable of such things, he considered.

'There is a smart way to determine this....' Inspector Boyle thought out loud to himself.'

'Yes? And what is that, Inspector?

'I trust we will keep this between the three of us and confined to these walls?'

Both men nodded their agreement, eager to hear the Inspector's theory.

'Very well – suppose we can arrange a meeting between the two gentlemen without Mr Haymer knowing? We could gauge by his reaction whether their business is amicable and then keep an eye on them both. If they are in it together, they are bound to talk at some point. Perhaps that's why this Pezzola chap was by the lake. That could be where they are due to meet?'

'But how would we arrange such a meeting without our suspicions being obvious and alerting them?' Mr Mckelvie queried.

'He has a point there, Inspector. If they are in it together then surely, they would smell a rat if we attempted to bring Mr Pezzola into the fray. He may well already be spooked by his encounter with the Colonel,' Doctor Carson said.

'Hmm, yes, that is the difficulty! Wait a second, I've got it!' Inspector Boyle clicked his fingers at the light bulb moment taking place in his head.

'Well?'

'Suppose Mr Haymer had to go to Oakford for something and we planned it in such a way that he would see Pezzola in passing, he would surely want to get a chance to talk to his companion, especially if their rendezvous was disturbed here at the Court? And, when he does, we could follow him discreetly.'

'It is a good idea, Inspector, but how would we get Mr Haymer to go to Oakford? It's hardly the weather for a jaunt and Oakford has near on nothing to entice a man of his character.'

'That, doctor, is where our trusty solicitor here comes in.'

'Me?!' Mckelvie spluttered, stunned.

'Yes, indeed, Mr Mckelvie. You are staying at the Hind's Head, aren't you? Well suppose you ask Mr Haymer to visit you there before you return to London, to arrange his inheritance – he's hardly going to find that suspicious.'

'It's actually quite brilliant!' Doctor Carson marvelled at the wily Inspector.

'I suppose that could work; yes, but how do we ensure Pezzola is also present?' Mckelvie interjected.

'That shouldn't be too difficult. I suspect if we could entice Mr Haymer to meet you early, we could arrange it so that he appears around Breakfast time. Pezzola is bound to come down for his meal and spot his former acquaintance.'

'You know, that actually could be the perfect trap! Alright, Inspector, I'm game,' Mckelvie agreed.

'Splendid. Before the afternoon is up, you will have to find time to speak to Mr Haymer and ask him to join you in the morning before you leave for your train.'

'I'll tell him I have some documents for him to sign, and that I would be keen to do his first thing in the morning in case he opted to go traveling once more! Should be no cause for alarm in that.'

'That's ideal, Mr Mckelvie,' Inspector Boyle said, proudly.

The three men finished their tea in silence, each satisfied that the trio was starting to unravel this mystery.

'What are we to do in the meantime, Inspector?' asked Doctor Carson, who was the first to break their silence.

'There is still value in continuing our interviews, doctor. Next, we shall speak to Miss Morris and the staff. Then, we will entrust Mr Mckelvie with laying his trap, and we will wait for the morning.'

'Leave it to me, Inspector! It's all rather exciting, quite the opposite to a day in my office,' Mckelvie mused.

'Indeed, it must be! Gentleman, in the words of Mr Sherlock Holmes, 'the game is afoot.' Boyle raised his teacup. It was the thrill of the hunt that made him glad he had opted for a career in the police force.

CHAPTER TWENTY TWO

The not so shy Lillie Morris

As soon as she entered the room, the Inspector realised Miss Morris was quite a beautiful young woman. Dainty and with a fresh, youthful complexion, she had a classic British femininity that was hard not to appreciate.

She came and sat on the sofa in front of the fireplace. The large piece of furniture made her look even more petite. Sitting with her hands entwined, she waited patiently and calmly for the Inspector to begin.

'Miss Morris, thank you for agreeing to see us.'

'I hardly think I was given any alternative,' she

said dryly, and in a tone, which suggested to the Inspector she was really much stronger than her tiny, delicate frame suggested.

'It is voluntary, Miss Morris, I assure you. There is no obligation to provide a statement at this time, but it may very well help us in our investigation.'

'Well, I certainly want to be as helpful as I can, Inspector – I definitely wouldn't want to be suspected of being involved in such a dreadful crime!'

'Oh, I hardly think we would suspect you, Miss Morris,' Doctor Carson said affectionately.

'Now, now, doctor – is a woman not capable of murder?!'

'I didn't mean to suggest…' he blushed.

'Relax, Doctor Carson, I'm just teasing.'

'Oh, good,' he sighed in relief.

'Perhaps we can begin by asking you to confirm your movements last night, Miss Morris?' Inspector Boyle intervened to spare the hapless doctor further embarrassment.

'Well, let's see, I was involved in a card game with Gerald, Mr Haymer, the Colonel and the good doctor here.'

'You were left, following the conclusion of that game, alone with Mr Haymer, weren't you?

'I was, Inspector, but I certainly hope you aren't insinuating anything inappropriate?'

It was Inspector Boyle's turn to blush, his cheeks turning an usual dark red, the sight of which gave great satisfaction to Miss Morris.

'I do enjoy making men uncomfortable, it's quite gratifying in its own way.'

'If we could continue...' Boyle had recovered his composure.

'Where were we? Ah, yes, my late-night escapades with Mr Haymer! Everyone else had left by 10pm, I recall. I wasn't tired and Mr Haymer was telling me of his travels around Africa. You see, I've always dreamt of seeing the world! Fowey is lovely but a part of me has always wanted to travel. I suspect it's Papa's artistic tendency to see the beauty of nature.'

'And how long did you remain in the library?'

'It could only have been 10 or 15 minutes. I was conscious I ought to check in on my stepmother. She has been out of sorts with a cold ever since we arrived. I suspect her brother's death brought about unhappy memories of Papa's loss too. She was very fond of Lord Avery, always spoke highly of him.'

'Where you fond of his lordship?'

'I barely knew him! I know he wasn't overly happy with Papa's career, felt it beneath the family! I resented him for a long time for that, but mama would always remind me of the good her brother had done to provide for us and as such, yes, I suppose I was fond of him. Perhaps, grateful is the right word!'

'I see, and then when you left the library, did you go straight to see your stepmother? What of Mr Haymer?'

'I said goodnight and he said he was going to remain downstairs and read for a while. So, I made my way up to mama's room, but she was sound asleep by that time. I didn't want to disturb her, so I made my way to my room and went to bed.'

'Did you sleep well?'

'Well, thank you for your concern, Inspector. Yes, I did! A good night on the whole, although I did hear a slight disturbance around 1am.'

'You did? What did you hear? Footsteps?' Once more Doctor Carson jumped the gun in his excitement. This time Boyle looked less impressed with his eager associate.

'Well, as a matter of fact, that is exactly what I heard! How could you possibly…. you heard it too, didn't you, doctor?!' she squealed.

'I did. I thought I was going crazy, hearing things, so I'm glad I'm not the only one.'

'I suppose we are united in our experience,' she beamed, causing him to feel the warmth on his cheeks rising once more.

'About these footsteps, Miss Morris, were they heavy? Soft? Could you tell which direction they went in?'

'Well, really, Inspector. Such things didn't even occur to me. I merely heard footsteps on the corridor, the old beams groaning, so I must have only been in a light sleep at the time! I paid no significance to the whole thing until you asked me just now! I hardly even connected it with Gerald's death.'

'Yes, of course, Miss, I merely wanted to ascertain as many of the facts as I could.'

'Of course, Inspector, is there anything else?'

'Just one thing, Miss. Were you aware of your cousin's uneasy feeling about becoming the next Lord Avery?'

'Why, yes, of course. He hardly shied-away from the fact! Before Doctor Carson here arrived yesterday, he was even bemoaning his bad luck to me and Richard.... bad luck is an understatement now!' she added, her voice trailing off.

'He said as much to you both? What was your reaction?' Boyle replied softly, his notebook poised in his hand.

'Well, naturally I tried to console him and reassure him he would make a wonderful Lord. Richard even remarked how it would be a privilege for anyone to have such an honourable title, although Gerald was less than impressed to hear that, especially from Richard.'

'Oh really? And why would that be?'

'As Gerald correctly pointed out, Richard had seldom expressed anything but his own distaste at the idea of being tied down by the expectations of a title in the past! It irked Gerald that he was trying to now make it sound so desirable.'

'Yes, I suppose it must have,' Boyle scribbled furiously in his notebook.

'Was there anything else said on the matter, Miss Morris?'

'I am afraid my use to you ends there, Inspector,' the young lady said, seemingly becoming quite uncomfortable with the whole process.

'And, you have been most helpful, Miss Morris, most helpful, indeed. Thank you for your time,' he smiled warmly at the young woman and watched her as she got up and left the room.

'A lovely, spirited creature, isn't she? Well, surely we now have further proof of our murderer moving around the house,' Doctor Carson exclaimed enthusiastically.

'I am not sure we have cause for celebration just yet, doctor. Miss Morris' information wouldn't hold up in a court of law!'

'Why the devil not?!'

'You led the witness, doctor! Unintentionally, I know, but regardless, you asked if she had *heard the footsteps*, thus planting this into her subconscious mind! We should be asking *what did you hear?* and then, if it matched your statement, we could be sure we were on the right track.'

Doctor Carson felt like a damned fool. He had all too often been a hindrance to the investigation and now, when they finally had secondary evidence to collaborate his own, it was inadmissible.

Inspector Boyle saw the dejected look on the younger man's face and felt he had perhaps chastised him too strongly. He wasn't overly bothered that the evidence wasn't usable, what mattered to him was that they had a clearer timeline of events, and that would help lead to the killer. He knew he had to make the doctor realise the error of his ways if he was to maintain a role as his aide in the investigation and, now he had done so, he hoped to relieve the younger man's sense of guilt.

'Don't be too downtrodden, doctor. It is encouraging that Miss Morris has provided a similar timestamp to events to yours, and it means we can say quite confidently that the killer was in the corridor just after 1am. If, in fact, this Mr Pezzola has a part to play in our little drama, we must now ask the question *how* he would have got into the house and when?'

'Well, surely Mr Haymer had the best opportunity to allow his accomplice in? He was left alone downstairs in the library and the sitting room next door has French doors leading out to the back lawn. It would have been a straightforward move,' Doctor Carson stated, eager to redeem himself.

'Yes, it does appear that way,' sighed Inspector Boyle, 'and yet, something tells me it isn't all that straightforward.'

The gleam in his eye was a tell-tale sign of his cognitive process, one which right now was working overtime.

CHAPTER TWENTY THREE

The trap is set

Mr Mckelvie had spent much of the last couple of hours going over what he needed to say to Mr Haymer. During the conversation with the Inspector and Doctor Carson, he had been so very enthusiastic about the idea of playing a leading role in trapping the potential murderer, it seemed almost thrilling. But now that he was alone and very soon to begin his part in the interrogation, he felt a sense of nervous dread. What if Haymer saw right through his ruse and he met a terrible end like poor old Gerald Avery?

'Ridiculous man! You're only asking him to meet you, not to hand over the murder weapon!' Mckelvie berated himself quietly as he sorted his things in his room, ready to make his way back to the village of Oakford and the relative sanctuary of Mrs Farley and the Hind's Head inn.

Packing the remaining papers into his briefcase, he descended the stairs, intending to bid goodbye to Lady Avery before bumping into an unsuspecting Richard Haymer in the library.

Plans, of course, seldom go as smoothly as one hopes and this was very much the case for Mr Mckelvie, as no sooner had he left his room and begun walking down the corridor than he came face-to-face with the very man.

'You're not leaving us are you, Mr Mckelvie?!' Haymer asked, in his usual charming tone.

'I am, I'm afraid, Mr Haymer. Business calls me back to London first thing tomorrow.'

'Well, that is a shame. It's awfully dull around here and it has been splendid having a few *normal* faces around to brighten up the day!'

Mr Mckelvie certainly didn't intend on continuing their idle chat for too long, especially as he felt his heart racing at a mile a minute.

'Before I forget, Mr Haymer, I must talk to you about your uncle's will.'

'Oh, yes?' the younger man's face seemed to stiffen.

'Nothing to worry about,' Mckelvie began, hoping his voice was hiding the nerves he felt. 'Just some paperwork that needs signing.'

'Ah I see, very well!' Haymer relaxed.

The sight of the younger man relaxing and buying into his story without an ounce of suspicion allowed Mr Mckelvie to steel himself and continue with a calmer disposition.

'Only I've left the paperwork over at the Hind's Head. I'm becoming an utter fool in my old age!' he continued, 'Would it be at all possible for you to join me there tomorrow morning before I depart for London? Figured it better to get it all in order with you in case you opted to go on another one of your most thrilling continental excursions!'

Richard Haymer took the bait, blissfully unaware. 'Why, certainly, Mr Mckelvie. I can come over at 8 if that suits? I do very much appreciate you being so diligent with this matter.'

'Not at all, Mr Haymer, not at all! We always pride ourselves on handling these matters as efficiently as possible! 8am will be ideal, thank you so much and please accept my sincere apologies for leaving those papers behind and making you drag out to Oakford.'

'Oh, think nothing of it, Mr Mckelvie, a bit of a break from this asylum will do me good. I must say I'm starting to get a bit of cabin fever holed up in here all day! It's a great relief that the snow is thawing at last.'

'It certainly is! Well I must be off now, Mr Haymer, see you tomorrow and thanks again!'

With that, Mckelvie made his way quickly down the corridor and to the staircase. As he descended, he breathed a sigh of relief, most pleased that the first part of the plan had gone without a hitch.

'Hook, line and sinker,' Mckelvie thought proudly to himself. 'I'm quite a natural at this acting malarkey.'

❊ ❊ ❊

The next morning, Mr Mckelvie was up bright and early. He had already packed his belongings as he did in fact intend to return to London following his orchestrated meeting with Richard Haymer.

As he made his way downstairs to the breakfast parlour of the Hind's Head, he wondered if Mr Pezzola might have already made his escape. After all, the Colonel had spotted him out in the trees, and this could very easily have frightened him off. He knew one thing for sure though; if there was any interesting gossip to be heard on the matter, it would surely come freely from the ever-present, all-seeing and all-hearing Mrs Farley.

'Morning, Mr Mckelvie, rest well did ya?' the landlady said in her thick country twang.

'I did, yes. Thank you, Mrs Farley.'

'I've got breakfast organised for you, can't have you heading off to London on an empty stomach!'

'That's awfully kind! I wonder if I might be able to use the telephone before I sit down to eat?'

'Of course, sir, it's through there, behind the bar.'

He bowed his head politely and made his way over to the telephone. From his vantage point, he could keep a clear eye on Mrs Farley and the staircase, ensuring he was able to speak freely without fear of being overheard.

On the third ring, the phone was picked up.

'Inspector Boyle here.'

'Hello good chap, it's me,' he replied eager to not say the Inspector's name.

'Mckelvie? That you?'

'Yes, that's right.'

'Is everything set?'

At that moment, Mrs Farley passed by, smiling innocently but evidently taking her time to leave the area.

'Yes, all is in order. I will be getting the 10am train back to London.'

'What are you on about man?' Boyle replied, thoroughly confused before the realisation hit him. 'That nosey spinster hanging about you?'

'Yes, that's it!' Mckelvie replied, grateful his need for discretion was ringing through.

'She really is a handful that one,' Boyle sighed. 'Still meeting Haymer at 8am?'

Once he had left Oakford Court the previous afternoon, Mckelvie had managed to pop by the Doctor's surgery and meet with his co-conspirators in peace. All satisfied that their plan was in motion, he had confirmed that the meeting would take place at 8am the following day at the Hind's Head.

Mercifully, Mrs Farley had been distracted by the arrival of the local greengrocer, making his rounds for the day, and had headed off, leaving Mckelvie in peace.

'She's gone now. Yes, he's coming here for 8. But Inspector, I've seen nothing of Mr Pezzola either yesterday evening or so far this morning – what if he's already left?'

'He hasn't. I've had ununiformed men at the train station since yesterday afternoon and he hasn't been there. So, unless he has managed to get a car, which we would know about, or trekked out in the snow, he is still in Oakford, don't you worry.'

'I suppose time will tell, as they say. Will you be on hand?'

'No, it would be too obvious if I were involved so I've asked one of my constables to be situated outside the tavern in plain clothes just in case he is needed, but it shouldn't come to that.'

Mr Mckelvie was impressed with the Inspector's efficiency but gulped at the thought of potential violence. It hadn't really dawned on him that he was about to become a sitting duck for a potential murderer and their accomplice. In that moment, he now couldn't help but wish for the peace and quiet of his home in London – of all the ironies!

'I will see you at the train station following your meeting. It will look like a pure coincidence we have bumped into each other and it will give you the chance to update me before you get on the train,' Inspector Boyle continued.

The plan was simple on paper, Mckelvie was to meet with an unsuspecting Haymer and when Pezzola came down for breakfast (a convenient phone call requesting him would be placed if needed), Mckelvie was to monitor the two men and look for clear signs of their knowing one another or attempting to communicate. Once all was sorted and Haymer had signed the papers

Mckelvie had managed to rustle up for him, he would then make his way to the station and update the Inspector. Mckelvie would then make his planned return to London and be free of the whole mess, at least he hoped!

Just then, he heard the tavern's large front door open, the sound of the wind beyond whirling through into the bar and, with it, in came Mr Richard Haymer.

'I best go now,' he said quietly into the receiver. 'My appointment is here.'

With that he put down the phone, steeled himself as best he could, and walked in the direction of Mr Haymer.

'Good morning, Mr Mckelvie,' the young man beamed, holding out a hand warmly.

'Good morning, Mr Haymer, thank you again for coming down to see me.'

'Not at all, it's nice to stretch the legs.'

The two men made their way into the lounge bar and seated themselves next to the fire, a place Mckelvie had deliberately chosen as it allowed him a prime location to see anyone else entering the room just before his guest would.

As they sat, Mrs Farley, fresh from her vocal debate with the greengrocer over the inadequate size of the apples he had provided, re-appeared and promptly approached the two men.

'Good morning, sir,' she bowed her head at the sight of Mr Haymer. 'Can I fetch you both a pot of tea?'

'That would be wonderful, thank you ever so much,' Haymer replied in his charming manner.

The old spinster was smitten by the younger man's attention and was, for perhaps one of the only times in her life, rendered speechless! Smiling, she shuffled away to get the tea.

'Am I to understand correctly from Lady Avery that you plan to stay in these parts for a while, Mr Haymer?'

'Ah, a bit of rotten luck that. I agreed on a whim so as not to disappoint my dear aunt, assuming I could simply make some excuse to go shortly afterwards - and then we had all this terrible business with Gerald.'

'Yes, it has been quite an unexpected few days.'

Richard Haymer nodded his agreement, a look of genuine sadness in his eyes, which, not for the first time, rendered Mr Mckelvie sceptical of his guilt.

'So, you do intend to stay for a while?'

'Yes, I suppose I ought to,' he sighed, 'help Aunt Ellen until this mess is cleared up.'

'Very noble of you.'

'I suspect I know why you've actually asked to

see me today.' Haymer said, his eyes fixed on the older man.

Mckelvie froze. Had he been rumbled? A thousand thoughts raced through his mind as he searched in vain for the appropriate response, praying his face hadn't given him up.

Before he could reply, Haymer smirked and continued: 'Yes, I thought something was awry! I can see it in your face.'

Mercifully, the reappearance of Mrs Farley with a large pot of tea gave Mr Mckelvie precious time to gather his thoughts. His head was spinning, and he longed for the help of Inspector Boyle. Should he call out for the Constable outside? *No, come on now, man*! He tried to calm himself, *let's see what he says first, he can't hurt you here.*

'Here we are, gentlemen, a nice pot of breakfast tea to warm your cockles as me old mam used to say!' Mrs Farley chuckled, pouring tea for Mr Haymer, who graciously accepted it.

'Thank you so much, you are quite a treasure!'

'Oh, sir, you flatter me,' she replied, blushing at the compliment as she turned to fill Mr Mckelvie's cup. 'And for you, Mr Mck…. oh, I say, sir, is everything alright?!'

'What? Oh, yes, yes quite fine. Thank you,' he spluttered in response, being brought firmly back into the moment.

'You scared me royally, sir! Looked like you'd seen a ghost!'

I'm afraid I might be to blame for Mr Mckelvie's look of shock, Mrs Farley, but fear not, I'm sure we will have it all sorted in no time.'

'Right you are, sir,' Mrs Farley bowed her head, looking concerned at the older of the two men as she made her retreat towards the kitchen.

'A nosey sort that one,' Haymer continued, sipping his tea. 'So then, Mr Mckelvie, shall we get down to the real purpose of this meeting?'

'Well, yes, but how, how did you know I had you here...'

'On false pretences? It doesn't take a genius to work that out, Mr Mckelvie!' Haymer smirked. 'As soon as poor Gerald was found and you asked to see me privately, I suspected it.'

'I suppose you would have, yes.' Mckelvie was shocked, but felt his fate was sealed now and waited for the younger man to continue.

'So, come on man, am I to be the new Lord of the Manor?! Is my fate decided against my will?'

Mr Mckelvie was astounded. He had utterly misread the entire situation, letting his nerves get the better of him. Haymer had no idea of the real reason he was here and, naturally, as the eldest son of the eldest born brother; he would be the natural heir following his cousin's untimely death and assumed as much. Mckelvie couldn't help but sigh in relief, the colour returning to his face as he relaxed his stiff posture in his chair.

'Of course, the heir!' he regathered his composure. 'Yes, you would be the next in line following poor Gerald's demise.'

'Ah I knew it! I knew that's why you called me here, away from the prying eyes of Oakford Court. You knew it was a burden I was damn sure I'd not want and you arranged to meet me privately, away from Aunt Ellen and the rest of them, to discuss my potential options, didn't you?!'

Mckelvie couldn't believe his luck. The younger man was quite literally giving him the perfect alibi for his trap and he instantly felt both utterly relieved and a little ashamed at being so flustered, , especially considering how grateful his guest was for his perceived help.

'Yes, you've got me! I wanted to talk to you alone about your late uncle's will and how you will now be likely to inherit the estate.'

'I feared as much. Mr Mckelvie, I'm not sure I am up for running the estate – never pictured myself having to lay down roots here in the motherland.'

'Naturally, Mr Haymer, but it would seem you are the only surviving heir of the paternal bloodline.'

Richard Haymer sighed heavily, his usual charmed glow fading fast as he became resigned to his destiny and contemplated the enormous burden on his shoulders.

'I suppose it really is my duty and to be Lord of the manor isn't the worst job a man could be lumped with,' he muttered, trying to convince himself more than Mckelvie.

'Oh, quite so, Mr Haymer, it is a privileged position that few in this country can ever dare dream of in their lifetime.'

'Hmm, yes, I suppose so. Well, I must honour my duty as my father would have wanted. What is the next move?'

'I will have to check my files in the office once I return to London, but if you can sign these documents it should be a formality in a couple of days or so.'

'Very well,' the young man said, duly taking the papers from the table in front of him and signing his name.

As he did so, Mckelvie saw a familiar figure emerging from the entrance to the lounge. It was the distinctive figure of Mr Pezzola.

The Italian had noticed his travelling companion long before arriving at the table and hadn't been able to see he wasn't alone. Mckelvie braced himself for the moment of truth as he came ever closer just as Haymer handed back the signed papers.

'Signor Mckelvie! I hear you are leaving us?' the Italian exclaimed in his usual dramatic way as he reached the table.

Just as he did so, he locked eyes with Mckelvie's guest occupying the high-backed chair alongside him. The look on Mr Pezzola's face was one of great surprise.

'May I introduce Mr Haymer to you, Mr Pezzola?' Mckelvie said, trying to remain as calm as possible as he eyed both men intently.

Richard Haymer's face turned a complete shade of ghostly white the instant he saw the Italian. There was a look in his eyes which surprised Mckelvie greatly as Haymer tried in vain to compose himself, standing and shaking hands with Pezzola.

'Why, no need to introduce us, signor. Me and Mr Haymer are past acquaintances,' Pezzola said, a sly smile appearing on his face.

Haymer was momentarily stunned before replying: 'Yes, gg...good to see you again, Pezzola.'

'The pleasure, signor, it is all mine! And now you must excuse me, gentlemen. I see I have interrupted your meeting and so I must say my adieu!' He bowed his head theatrically. 'Signor Mckelvie, I wish you well for the future and, Mr Haymer, it has been a most enlightening experience to remake your acquaintance.'

Before either man could respond, the Italian swiftly departed as his attention turned to the lingering presence of Mrs Farley.

'A colourful character that Mr Pezzola! I didn't realise you knew him, a small world eh!' Mckelvie said as light-heartedly as he could, his eyes fixated on the man sat opposite him.

'Yes.... quite small, indeed.' Haymer struggled to respond, his faced glazed over as if he were in deep thought.

'How did the two of you meet?' Mckelvie probed further, casually.

Haymer seemed to pull himself together and some level of composure regained itself in his manner. 'Well, let's see. We met out on the continent. He's a salesman of some sort and I think we must have met each other at one of the Marquis of Sicily's lavish balls.'

'How fascinating a life, you lead, Mr Haymer.'

'Yes, well it certainly sounds that way but rest assured, Mr Mckelvie, my life is not that much different to yours or any other man's,' he said in a tone which was not entirely believable.

'I hardly think my life in a London office can compare with your rambles around the world!'

'Well, I suppose I am quite lucky!' He checked his watch, 'I say! It's nearly 9.15! I wouldn't want to make you miss your train, Mr Mckelvie.'

'Ah, I suppose I ought to get myself ready for the return journey, yes. Thank you for taking the time to come down, Mr Haymer, and once my firm has had the opportunity to check the paperwork thoroughly and make the necessary arrangements, we will be in touch. I trust you'll be staying at the Court?'

'Oh yes, Mr Mckelvie, I hardly suspect I can leave just yet!'

'Jolly good, well let me walk you to the door.'

With that, Mr Mckelvie followed the younger man to the door and extended a hand to him.

'Good luck, Mr Haymer. I'm sure all will be fine once we have everything in order.'

Haymer shook his hand, opened the large tavern door and replied: 'Thank you, Mr Mckelvie, I look forward to having things finalised as soon as we can. No sense putting Aunt Ellen through any further undue stress.'

'Oh, quite so, quite so. Good day, Mr Haymer.'

With that the younger man nodded, pulled his coat collar high around his neck and stepped out into the cold air. As Haymer began to walk away, Mckelvie watched him through the window discreetly, observing as young Richard Haymer stopped and stared intently at a window high up on the second floor of the old tavern. The same look appeared on his face as Mckelvie had seen earlier, and the realisation struck him that the look he saw was one of sheer terror.

CHAPTER TWENTY FOUR

A meeting of minds on the train

As Mr Mckelvie approached Oakford station, he noticed two men stood at the entrance, both seemingly reading their newspapers – and, yet, neither was actually focused on the paper outstretched in front of them. Instead, they were both focused on him.

He walked towards them, keeping his head low as he carried his small suitcase alongside him. As he got closer, one of them, still reading the paper, spoke: 'Mr Mckelvie?'

'Yes?' he said looking directly at the man.

'Keep looking forward, sir. The Inspector is in the third carriage. He is expecting you, added the non-descript man without glancing up from his paper. It was only then that Mckelvie recognised him as one of Boyle's officers.

Mr Mckelvie realised the need for discretion and continued his walk into the station and out onto the lone platform. It was hardly busy this time of year, save a couple of people being helped onto the train by porters.

Making his way onto the third carriage, he glanced down the compartments and saw the distinctive look of the Inspector ushering him in. Once he was in the compartment, Inspector Boyle pulled the curtain across and locked the door.

'Apologies for the espionage, Mr Mckelvie, but I have to be sure we can talk in private.'

'It's alright Inspector – truth be told, I'm pleased to be away from Oakford.'

The train started its slow, lumbered departure from the station and their journey began in earnest.

'Well, what happened? Were we right, do they know one another?' Boyle leaned forward in anticipation.

'Oh yes, they certainly have met before, there's no doubt about that. They both said as much.'

'Well, I say!'

'But it wasn't at all how I expected it would be.'

'How so?'

'It's the queerest thing. When they both set eyes on one another, they had very separate and distinctive reactions, which differed from man to man.'

'How bizarre! Now think carefully, Mr Mckelvie. The more detail you can provide the better,' Boyle said, his pen poised in hand over his ever-present notebook.

'Well, firstly Mr Pezzola – when he first saw Haymer - he looked genuinely shocked, as if he hadn't expected to see him at all.'

'That's normal. He was hardly expecting his accomplice to be turning up – that was the whole point of our little ruse.'

'No, there was more to it than that! He seemed genuinely shocked to see the man at all, as if he hadn't for some time. 'Plus, he relaxed almost as quickly. There was no sign of guilt or panic at seeing Haymer.'

'Now that is odd. He is either an exceptional actor or else he surely can't be concerned about seeing Haymer, which would suggest innocence.'

'That's the quandary,' Mckelvie agreed.

'Well, what about Haymer, you said his expression was very different?'

'Now, that is where it truly gets interesting. I couldn't quite put my finger on it at first, but there was a distinct look in his eyes, and it was only later that it dawned on me – it was a look of fear.'

'Ha! Now that is a much guiltier trait! And yet you don't look convinced, Mr Mckelvie?!'

'No, I must confess, I'm not. He was fearful of Mr Pezzola, it seemed. He was utterly dumbfounded to see the Italian and I hardly think he had set eyes on the man in years.'

'Hmm, that does make for quite a twist in our theory,' Boyle pondered, writing notes in his notebook.

'What does it all mean?'

'Well, let's review the facts as you have witnessed them,' Boyle replied, flicking to the relevant page in his notebook, before adding: '

1. Pezzola is travelling to Cornwall on business and stops in Oakford for the weekend.

2. Haymer is brought home by his uncle's death.

'With this in mind, the questions we need to answer become:

1. Pezzola - Why Oakford? Does he know

Haymer is here?

2. Haymer - Does he know Pezzola is here? If not, why would he be scared to see this person from his past?

3. If neither man knows the others is here – is one of them the murderer? If not, who is?'

Mr Mckelvie listened intently and sat a moment in silence before offering the only reply he could.

'So, with these questions, what do we do next?

'That is the mystery we are now faced with. I confess, the pieces were beginning to fit into the little puzzle I've been trying to solve in my mind. But this development does change things somewhat,' Boyle said, looking less assured than usual.

'I don't envy your job, Inspector,' Mckelvie chuckled as he gazed out of the window at the passing scenery.

The train was slowing once more as it began its approach to the next station.

'It is not a profession for the weakhearted,' Inspector Boyle agreed, 'but this is my stop, Mr Mckelvie!'

'You're leaving already?'

'Oh yes, I must get back to Oakford and set in

motion the next steps of the investigation without a moment's delay. This little trip of mine was a fact-finding mission, and your help has been of the greatest significance.'

Mckelvie blushed, not expecting such a compliment from the Inspector.

'Thank you, Inspector Boyle, I am only sorry I couldn't aid you further.'

'There might still be time yet,' Boyle chuckled as he stood, shaking hands warmly with his companion. 'For now, safe travels, Mr Mckelvie. I assure you; we will keep you abreast of developments and please do the same if anything lands on your desk.'

As Mckelvie watched Inspector Boyle descend from the train carriage and move briskly to the waiting car driven by his faithful Constable, he recalled something Boyle had said on the train about the profession of a detective not being for the weakhearted.

'That is certainly not a weakhearted man,' Mckelvie mused.

CHAPTER TWENTY FIVE

Poor Mr Tiddlesworth

Doctor Carson had waited anxiously for news from Inspector Boyle, following his meeting with Mr Mckelvie on the train. The phone call had come through to him in his surgery shortly before midday and now he found himself most confused by the latest developments.

Like Mckelvie, he had serious doubts over Richard Haymer's guilt, and it would appear the evidence supported that. But another mystery was unfolding, who was this Giuseppe Pezzola and how did he fit into the picture surrounding Gerald Avery's murder?

The Inspector had asked to meet with him later that afternoon to go through their next steps and he had agreed to do so the moment he had finished with his daily appointments. So far, his patients had made up the usual old biddies that saw their weekly appointment at the surgery as more of a social event than a healthcare necessity. First came widowed Mrs Christie, a lively woman of 83 years whose only real ailment was her own paranoia. She was in extremely good health for her age and still maintained an active social life as head of the village horticultural society, and as a frequent presence on the bowls green. Yet, she insisted on seeing the doctor as a matter of urgency as soon as the mildest tickle rose in her throat!

His second appointment of the day was a house call to see poor old Mr Stewart. A retired schoolteacher and lifelong Oakford resident, Stewart was bedridden and in the throngs of a vicious bout of pneumonia. In just his late 60's, Doctor Carson still suspected he would be the next of his patients to meet their maker and, with the harsh winter in full force, he supposed it wouldn't be long.

Next up, he had seen Miss Lightwood, a lifelong spinster whose focus was entirely on her cats, whom she doted on as warmly as if they were her own children. Unlike the hypochondriac Mrs Christie, she was a stubborn old woman who seldom left her home except for groceries or visits to the vet. Her home was a small cottage on the outskirts of the village, and, during the summer months, it represented a picturesque example of a quaint village home with its white picket fence, smart floral displays and thatched roof. Yet, in the midst of winter, it presented a dour façade, isolated from the small community down the way.

A young girl from the village was employed in service for the old spinster and Miss Lightwood took every opportunity to bemoan the girl's inability to successfully perform any menial task.

'Doctor, I simply must apologies for Daisy's utter inability to cater for our guests in a timely manner.'

'Oh, there is no need to go to any trouble, Miss Lightwood.'

'Nonsense – if I've told her once, I've told her a thousand times! Daisy!' she bellowed, causing one of her many cats to jump from its slumber on her lap. 'Oh, now look what she's done, poor Mr Tiddlesworth.'

The young girl came rushing into the front room of the small cottage, flustered as she held onto a feather duster tightly.

'Yes, Miss Lightwood?'

'Daisy, the doctor is an extremely busy man and

I hardly think he has time to wait for you to finish dusting before bringing through the tea and biscuits!'

Doctor Carson dared not point out that as an extremely busy medical man, he hardly had time to sit and have tea with a housebound spinster.

'Sorry, Miss Lightwood. I've been dusting the pictures as you asked.'

'That should have been completed this morning. I should hardly have to remind you of your priorities!'

Yes, of course, Miss Lightwood, I'll fetch the tea now.'

'Such a daft girl – I really had such rotten luck being landed with her.'

Again, Doctor Carson bit his lip. He thoughtfully considered that it was actually poor Daisy who'd drawn the short straw in their relationship.

'Well, Miss Lightwood, the good news is that your temperature has come right down - I would suggest a couple more days of rest and you'll make a full recovery.'

'Bah! I told that silly girl not to fuss!'

'Daisy was right to call me over last week, Miss Lightwood. You need to be extremely cautious of colds at your....' His voice petered off, eager not to offend the cantankerous old woman.

'At my what, doctor? My age? People get so worked up with age these days – it's all a load of poppycock! Why, I shouldn't be surprised if I live till a hundred!

Doctor Carson blushed and replied diplomatically: 'Yes, quite so, forgive me.' Although the thought of Miss Lightwood living to be 100 wouldn't surprise him at all, not because of her health but more likely so she could continue to traumatise poor Daisy, who'd no doubt remain trapped with her.

'About time! I wondered if we'd see Spring before that tea arrived!' Miss Lightwood quipped as Daisy re-emerged from the kitchen, nervously carrying a tray with the best china trembling away.

'Thank you, Daisy,' Carson said kindly, taking his china cup from the young girl, who smiled gratefully for the kind response.

As she passed the cup to her employer though, the response was far less civil.

'Oh, do be careful you silly child, that tea is likely to spill all over me!'

'Ss...sorry, Miss Lightwood.'

Leaving the biscuits on the small table in-between their two chairs, the timid young maid made her way from the room, but not before having another instruction barked in her direction.

'Now, don't forget to dust the bannisters, Daisy!' Miss Lightwood moaned, before her tone became instantaneously more amicable as she turned her attention back to the doctor. 'Now then, do tell me how the investigation at Oakford Court is going, doctor.'

He shuffled awkwardly in his seat; conscious he must find a way to placate the old lady's nosiness without revealing crucially important details from their ongoing investigation.

'Well, I couldn't really say. I have been only a casual observer in the matter due to my profession and the fact I was in the house at the time, but beyond that I wouldn't like to say I have any details to share.'

'Nonsense, doctor! I hear you have been acting in a deputy role to Inspector Boyle himself on the matter.'

Carson cursed the gossipy nature of the small village; it was foolish to assume that anyone could keep a secret for too long.

'Well, it is true that I have been aiding the Inspector, but I can assure you, Miss Lightwood, that all efforts are being made to ensure we resolve the matter as quickly as possible.'

'Oh, I have no doubt of that doctor. Inspector

Boyle is a most efficient man, I am told.' The old lady nodded happily to herself.

How she came to such a conclusion or who had highlighted the Inspector's merits to her were not forthcoming.

'His reputation certainly precedes him.'

'It's a terrible case, really,' Miss Lightwood continued. 'Lady Avery is a strong woman but to lose both your husband and your only child in such a manner really must have taken its toll.'

'She is handling things remarkably well. I must confess she impresses me greatly with her strength,' Carson agreed.

'Has the murder weapon been found yet, doctor?'

Doctor Carson nearly spat out his tea in utter shock. 'How on earth did you know it was missing? That is something that only a handful of people were privy to.'

Miss Lightwood chuckled to herself as she leant forward and took a custard cream from the small array of biscuits.

'Come now, doctor, you've lived here long enough to know there is are few secrets in Oakford! Besides, when you've had as long a life as mine, one always seems to have gossip fall upon them.'

'It's quite extraordinary! This really isn't information that needs to be shared about. We are, Miss Lightwood, still searching for the weapon and any idle gossip to its whereabouts will greatly hamper our efforts.' His tone was sterner, born of frustration momentarily, before remembering he was a guest of the elderly lady. Sinking back into his chair, he took a long sip of his tea awaiting a potential backlash.

'You are quite right, doctor, and naturally, I wouldn't be one to gossip myself.' she replied more seriously – ignoring the total absurdity of her statement.

'No, quite so.'

'I am sure the weapon will be found in due course. Inspector Boyle is very capable indeed and, when you have an old place like Oakford Court, there are plenty of hiding places to make the job altogether more difficult. Why, there are all those secret tunnels for a start!'

'Secret what?!' Carson exclaimed.

'The secret tunnels – surely you knew about those, doctor?!' she replied, bewildered by his sudden surprise.

'I've never heard anything of the sort!'

'Oh, well Oakford Court has several secret passageways which were built during the Great War, I believe. My niece, Sarah, was a maid there before her wedding and she saw them firsthand!'

'I say! Do you know where these tunnels are?!' His pulse raced at the possibility there was areas of the old Court unbeknown to them.

'Not personally. But she said they ran beneath the house and down to the grounds beyond as I recall.'

The doctor was on his feet at once, placing his cup down with a slightly greater force than he anticipated and very nearly leaving another stain for poor Daisy to contend with.

'Miss Lightwood, I am sorry to depart suddenly but I must go at once.'

The old lady wasn't altogether shocked by the doctor's actions. She had, after all, seen plenty of hasty exits from her cottage over the years, although she assumed this was more due to the bizarre nature of her guests rather than her own challenging personality.

'Already doctor? Why, that is a shame, but please do come back soon and let me know how you get on with those passages.'

He gave a wry smile at the wily old lady and nodded politely as he made his hasty exit.

His rounds were seldom joyful. More often than not, they were a journey filled with stories of sickness and discomfort but, today, proved to be very different. Today, his rounds had set him upon an exciting new lead, one he felt confident could help crack the case. A visit to Miss Lightwood was usually one that filled him with dread and yet, today, he couldn't have been happier to have seen the old battleaxe. She may just have provided the missing piece of the puzzle.

❊ ❊ ❊

Doctor Carson didn't waste any time after leaving Miss Lightwood's. It was a fresh afternoon, and the daylight was fading fast, yet his walk through the village to the local police station didn't take long and, mercifully, he didn't pass anybody who was likely to delay him. It was always a rare joy when he made it across Oakford without one of his patients blindsiding him with questions on their various ailments. Most turned out to be nothing more than paranoia, and yet by the time he had reassured them sufficiently, he could have lost the best part of half an hour. Today, though, the impending dusk and cold air ensured he made it directly to the station house alongside the old churchyard without interruption.

The station itself was a small house differentiated from the others only by the blue glass lamp outside proudly illuminating the word 'Police' upon it. As he opened the front door and made his way into the small reception lobby, he was greeted by the local constable, a young and uninspiring type by the name of Jackson.

'Good afternoon, Jackson.'

'Anything the matter, doctor?' the young man asked, his boredom momentarily lifted by the idea that he might finally have something to do other than mundane desk work.

'No, no, I am here to see Inspector Boyle. I believe he is expecting me?'

'Oh, right,' Jackson's mood faltered, resigned, as it was, to returning to a state of boredom. 'Please go through. He is using the room to the left.'

'Thank you, Jackson.'

Passing the young man, who by this time had returned to the small pile of paperwork set out in front of him, Carson made his way through the hallway and towards the office on the left hand side, which he suspected would have once been the lounge space of the former house. Knocking firmly on the oak door, he awaited a response.

'Come.'

Opening the large door, he entered the room and found Inspector Boyle sat behind a large mahogany desk lined with large piles of paperwork on either side. The sight of the doctor instantly improved his mood.

'Ah, doctor! I trust all went well with your

rounds?'

'Yes, thank you, Inspector! In fact, it has been a most productive afternoon.'

Something in the doctor's tone told Boyle that his excitement was based on far more than just an afternoon free of any serious decline in his elderly patients' health.

'I assume something of note has happened?'

'Indeed, it has! I have just come from old Miss Lightwood's house, a most insufferable woman usually, who will no doubt live forever despite her own adamant belief she is at death's door.'

Inspector Boyle chuckled warmly. He was aware of her sort. His line of work often led him to such houses to meet similar insufferable types.

'I believe every village in England has a Miss Lightwood, eh, doctor!'

'Yes, quite so!' Carson laughed, 'but this visit was memorable for all the right reasons! You see, it seems we may have overlooked a key part of Oakford Court in our search for the dagger.'

'Overlooked, you say?! But how? We have looked through the entire house and grounds.'

'Evidently not, Inspector. –Miss Lightwood informs me that there is a series of secret passageways under the old house, built during the Great War.'

Boyle raised an eyebrow at the revelation and leaned forward in his chair.

'And, you believe this, doctor? How reliable is this Miss Lightwood?'

Doctor Carson took a moment to ponder the question. In his haste to have a new lead, he hadn't stopped to ask the question of whether the old spinster's statement could be true or simply a figment of your imagination.

'Truthfully, I am not sure now that you mention it. I have spent enough time with old spinsters in this village to know they embellish tales and local folklore still holds a lot of sway in their memories.'

'Well, that's not unusual, but in my experience there's a lot to be said for the tales passed down from generation to generation,' Boyle replied, entirely seriously. 'So, ignoring the logic, what does your gut tell you about her belief?'

'I am inclined to believe she is telling the truth. She told me her niece worked there many years ago before her marriage and had seen the tunnels herself. I see no reason for her to lie about such things.'

Inspector Boyle clasped his hands together beneath his chin and reclined slightly and thoughtfully in his creaking chair. A moment passed in which he seemed completely engrossed in a far-off thought process before giving his reply.

'I agree with your sentiment, doctor. There is no reason for this old bird to lie about such things and, with that in mind, it means we have yet to complete our inspection of the Court. IF, there are secret tunnels, I would wager that Harley is sure to know about them, and it begs the question why weren't they mentioned when we were exploring the property before?'

'It does seem rather peculiar that he wouldn't mention it,' Carson agreed, nodding.

'Well, I see no other course of action but to return to the Court at once and see if we can locate these passageways.'

With that, Boyle sprung from his chair and grabbed his coat from the rack to the side of the door, leaving Carson to scramble behind him as they made their way to the entrance hall where young Jackson was slumped in his chair, seemingly nodding off.

'Look lively boy!' Boyle quipped as the young officer jumped in surprise.

'Sorry, sir!' Jackson muttered, his cheeks turning a shade of crimson.

'We must go to Oakford Court at once, bring round the car.'

'Aye, sir!' Jackson's face lit up – finally he was going to get into the action and escape his tedious desk duties which had plagued him over the previous few days.

Within a few short minutes, the three of them were making the short journey out of the village and towards the imposing gothic abode of Oakford Court, a house whose secrets it seemed were growing greater all the time.

CHAPTER TWENTY SIX

The plot thickens

Upon arrival at the Court, Inspector Boyle had immediately instructed Harley to join them in the sitting room. The old butler was initially startled by their reappearance and interest in seeing him, rather than the lady of the house.

'Me, sir? I think her ladyship should be notified of receiving guests at this hour.'

The hour was a little after 6pm and whilst it was now entirely dark outside, Boyle hardly suspected her ladyship would mind their unexpected presence.

'Please do let her ladyship know we are here,

Harley, and that the purpose of our visit is to follow up on a potential new lead in our investigation, which we would like to discuss with you.'

'A new lead? Very good, sir. If you would like to wait in the sitting room, I shall notify her of your arrival.' The butler seemed to turn an even paler shade of white at the Inspector's insistence that they speak to him, but maintaining his composure, dutifully made his way to inform Lady Avery.

When they were once more alone, Doctor Carson commented on the butler's nervous disposition.

'Harley seemed rather unsettled when you mentioned we had a new lead to discuss with him specifically.'

'Yes, he did – even more reason to ensure we talk to him tonight, while we have the element of surprise over this new information,' Boyle stated, before turning his attention to Jackson. 'Now, listen here lad, we need to ensure we cover all areas of this house, but if you find anything of interest, do not touch it without my knowing, you hear?'

'Yes, sir,' Jackson nodded enthusiastically, evidently thrilled to be in the heart of a murder investigation.

With that matter settled, the three men each

found themselves instinctively looking around the room in even more detail than they had previously. The wood panelling covered half the walls, and the remainder were wallpapered and covered in grand pieces of art – a collection of natural scenes in oil. Carson ran his hands along the panelling hoping to find a subtle break which could lead to a secret passageway, but nothing at all seemed out of the ordinary.

Harley appeared moments later, silently entering the room and almost causing Jackson to jump out of his skin.

'Lady Avery would like me to relay to you that you are most welcome to use the court as you see fit this evening, gentlemen, on the condition that you meet with her before you leave. With this in mind, I am, therefore, at your service, Inspector.'

'That's very kind of her ladyship, and thank you too, Harley. Please do take a seat.'

The butler sat on an armchair facing the Inspector and Doctor Carson, whilst Jackson stood quietly at the doorway awaiting further instructions.

'It has come to our attention, Harley, that there may be passageways within the Court that we have yet to investigate as part of our enquiries,' Boyle began, watching the butler's face closely.

'Passageways, sir?' the butler enquired, his face remaining stoic.

'Secret passageways,' Boyle replied as a matter of course.

Once again there seemed to be a complete lack of emotion on the butler's face as he calmly replied.

'Well, there are a couple of small passageways, sir, but I would hardly call them *'secret'*. But I wouldn't imagine they have been looked at in over 30 years.'

'So, you are aware of their existence and didn't think to mention them when we were searching the property?'

'It really didn't cross my mind, sir. As I say, to the best of my knowledge they haven't been opened in many years and were nothing more than a novelty Lord Avery's father had incorporated into the property as a party piece to impress his guests.'

'Harley, these passageways could very well be hiding our missing murder weapon,' Boyle replied sternly.

Despite his many years of handling the demanding and often unpredictable nature of the social elite, even Harley felt a rush of shame at his oversight.

'I am so sorry, sir. Please accept my sincerest

apologies and know I wouldn't deliberately withhold such information from you, if I had contemplated such a thing.'

Boyle softened his approach, realising the old butler could very well have genuinely forgotten the passageways. In any case, whether he had or not really wasn't the point at this moment in time. They had come to confirm the existence of the passages and having spoken to the butler, they simply had to investigate them firsthand.

'It's OK, Harley. These things happen, but perhaps you can show us where the passages are so we can review them ourselves without any further delay?'

Again, the butler seemed uneasy, shifting in his seat.

'I can show you two of them, sir, but the third one, I'm afraid, I wouldn't know how to access.'

'What?!' Doctor Carson gasped.

'It is a family tradition that the master's study remains solely for the lord of the house and, as such, whilst I know a passageway exists in that room, I haven't ever been given access to it or know how to locate it.'

'It seems we take two steps back every time we feel we're making progress!' Doctor Carson despaired.

'Such is the nature of detective work, doctor!'

Boyle said, a wry smile on his face. 'Besides, it's not all bad! We can start with the other two passageways and then try the study.'

'I suppose we at least know the room in which to look,' Carson stated, still dejected.

'Now, that's more like it! Saves us plenty of time for certain! Harley, we will follow you.'

'Very well, sir, we shall begin with the drawing room.'

The group followed the elderly man into the room and stood expectantly as he made his way over to the large ornate marble fireplace on the left-hand side.

With seemingly great effort, he pushed at the sculpted figure on the left-hand column and, sure enough, it began to sink into itself. The fireplace moved aside just enough for them to enter one by one.

'Right, go ahead Jackson,' Boyle started, indicating for the young officer to take the lead.

'Me, sir?' Jackson replied meekly, looking less than thrilled at the prospect.

'Yes, come along now.'

Jackson edged reluctantly towards the passageway, peered inside and cautiously entered.

'Well?' Boyle called after him, as his figure was no longer visible.

'It's too dark, sir. I can barely see my hand in front of my face.'

'Harley, do you have a lantern or candle we could use?'

'Certainly, sir.'

The butler left the room, returning just a moment later with a small candle in a holder.

Jackson was given the light and proceeded to examine the passageway.

'It's very small in here, sir, shouldn't imagine there's enough space for more than two of us to be in at one time.'

'Do you see anything of note, Jackson?' Doctor Carson called into the void.

'Not really, doctor, just a lot of cobwebs and a couple of empty wooden crates but nothing else.'

'Crates?' Boyle asked, leaning into the void himself.

'Yes, sir, but they're empty.' Jackson lifted one up to show the Inspector.

'What did I tell you about touching things, lad?!' Boyle barked, causing Jackson to curse himself.

'Sorry, sir.'

'It's done now and if they are empty, hopefully, no harm is done - but please be more careful next time.'

'Yes, sir. Sorry, sir.' Jackson said, following his superior out of the passageway before helping Harley push back the figure on the mantle to return the fireplace to its intended position.

'Those crates mean anything to you, Harley?'

'I believe Lord Avery's father had a wine collection that he was known to keep around the Court, sir. Perhaps it is remnants of that?'

'That does seem logical, yes. Well. where to next?'

'The other passageway is in the library, sir.'

As they made their way into the library and began scanning the bookshelves, Harley diverted their attention to a particularly old volume, bound in red leather, which looked to be in remarkable shape when compared to those around it.

'This is the one,' he said, pulling the book towards him at a 90-degree angle. As he did so, the entire bookcase made a loud groan and swung ever so slightly towards them.

The passageway seemed a little wider this time and, one by one, they were able to enter, following the nervous Jackson, still holding the candle out in front of him. Unlike the other passage, this one was, in fact, a tunnel which carried on for some 200 metres before they hit a dead end.

'Why does it just stop so abruptly, I wonder?' Carson asked.

Once more, Harley came to their rescue with the answer.

'It was said, sir, that this tunnel was being constructed during the Great War as an escape route from the Court. Originally, it was to lead all the way to the great fountain on the lawn but, during the dig, the war finished, and the lord turned his attentions to cultivating the rose gardens.'

'This isn't looking promising so far, especially when you consider the third and final tunnel could prove impossible to find, let alone access.' Doctor Carson was becoming increasingly frustrated by their searches for the lost weapon and, for once, the others did little to argue with his notion.

As they made their way back to the library, in relative silence, they closed off the passageway and stood waiting for Inspector Boyle to determine their next step.

'Gentlemen, we have started this little endeavour and however disappointing the outcome has proven thus far, we simply cannot leave without finding that final passageway. I propose then that we go to the master's study and do what we can to locate the entrance.'

Jackson and Doctor Carson nodded their agreement, but Harley cleared his throat and replied, 'I hope you don't mind, sir, but I must be returning to my duties in time for dinner service.'

'Of course, Harley, thank you for your assistance with this. All I would ask is you let us into the master's study and notify Lady Avery. I will be at her disposal in due course.'

'Certainly, sir,' the old butler replied, steering the group towards the staircase and up to the top floor of the old mansion.

'Has this room been used at all recently, Harley?' Boyle enquired as they ascended the final narrow staircase and found themselves on a small, terraced landing.

'Other than when your officers inspected the property, sir, this room hasn't been used for some time. Lord Avery couldn't be left alone in the last few weeks and had constant care from the nurses and staff in his bedroom quarters.'

'I see – when would he have last used this particular room, if you can recall that?'

'I can, sir. Lord Avery was last in here a month ago. He had requested that nobody disturb him, not even Lady Avery, as he had a pressing issue to attend to at his desk.'

'Was that in any way out of the ordinary?' Carson interjected.

'His lordship often preferred his privacy, as did

his father before him. The master's study was their sanctuary within the house, and everyone was instructed to leave the lord to his own company during his time there. Often, this would be for several hours.'

'And on this final occasion, he was left for roughly how long?'

'Let me see. I remember it was after dinner, sir, that he informed me he was going to write some important letters in his study and that under no circumstance was he to be disturbed. This would have been around 7pm, and he then rang for me around 11pm from his bedroom, which was the next time I or any of the staff saw him.'

'Interesting,' Boyle made another note in his notebook. 'That will be all, Harley, thank you.'

'Very good, sir.'

With that, the old butler turned on his heels and departed back down the stairs. His light frame meant that hardly a single noise was heard from his descent down the aged wooden staircase.

Inspector Boyle led the way into the master's study and took stock of the room laid out in front of him. It was a large room with a huge semi-circular window which provided beautiful views over the grounds far below. To the left-hand side was a single fireplace, consisting of dark oak with a green marble surround. Directly opposite this was the lord's writing desk. Still piled high with papers and books, the desk had a single lamp sat on top of it alongside a picture of a much younger Lady Avery perched by a large tree.

The rest of the room was an assortment of the late lord's collection of trinkets; statues and hunting trophies from his time on the continent, all of which, were dotted around in an unorganised mess.

'Blimey! You can tell this room was only for the man of the house,' Jackson piped up, moving in behind Boyle.

'And what brings you to that conclusion, Jackson?' Boyle replied, 1 unimpressed that the young officer felt the need to voice an opinion.

'It's just the layout, sir,' Jackson began, his cheeks reddening as he regretted his previous exuberance. 'It's dysfunctional and messy. Certainly not something you see from a woman's influence.'

Doctor Carson waited to hear the Inspector's retort and expected it to be more brutal than, in fact, it was.

'I suppose you're right, Jackson. Although need I remind you, we are looking for vital evidence in the murder case. We aren't here to judge Lord Avery's cleaning routine!'

Jackson hung his head to shield his embarrassment. 'Yes, sir. Sorry again, sir.'

Satisfied that the junior officer had received the appropriate dressing down, Boyle proceeded to move towards the desk and instructed Doctor Carson and Jackson to inspect the room closely. The desk, although strewn with papers, personal letters, and documents, was in fact very uninteresting. From what Inspector Boyle could gauge, the lord's elongated writing sessions focused more on his responses to journalists whose newspaper articles he had taken offence to or queries with art dealers who were ignoring his requests for clarity to the origins of various pieces in his possession.

'Anything looking out of the ordinary, Jackson?'

'Not yet, sir. I have been looking through the various piles of trinkets and possessions, but it all seems pretty normal so far.'

'What about you, doctor?'

'I must confess I've had no luck so far, Inspector. I rather fancied this fireplace would hold a secret lever much like the one down in the drawing room but, alas, it all seems utterly solid.'

'We know there is another passageway leading off this room, so there has to be a lever somewhere,' Boyle replied, urging the men on.

The three of them continued their search for another five minutes without a single indication of another passageway existing. Whilst none of them dared suggest it out loud, each man was beginning to doubt that a third chamber even existed when Jackson, busy running his hand across one of the wall panels, tripped on the tiger skin rug under foot and plunged forward. Desperate to avoid falling flat on his face, his outstretched arm collided with an ornate oriental vase sitting on the floor to the side of the desk, causing it to rock violently and move ever so slightly out of position.

'Blast it, man! If you break anything, you'll be paying for it!' Boyle lambasted.

'Sorry, sir,' Jackson muttered as he regained his composure.

Doctor Carson ignored the Inspector's dressing down of his colleague because his attention was focused on the part of the floor now visible where the vase had moved from its long-held position.

'I say, what's that?' he gasped bending down to examine the floor.

Boyle, whose attention had been firmly distracted by the clumsy young officer, turned to see what Carson was looking at.

'Have you found something, doctor?'

'I believe I have, at least…it looks like it.'

Boyle moved over and crouched down next to the doctor, who by this point was trying to move the vase further from its original location, revealing a small square cut out in the wooden floor panels.

'You're right, doctor! It's a hidden cavity.'

The two men moved the large vase off the remainder of the square and pulled up the loose bit of floorboard to reveal a small cavity of about 6 inches. Sat within the void was a small lever.

'Incredible! Should we pull it?' Carson asked, the excitement in his voice rising at the find.

'Of course, we should!'

'Right - well, here goes nothing.'

As he slowly pulled on the iron lever, the wood panel to the side of the large window opened slightly to reveal an entrance, similar to the one they had seen in the library.

'You did it, doctor!' Boyle exclaimed, slapping his compatriot heartily on the back.

'Well, actually, Inspector, without Jackson, I doubt we'd have ever found the lever.'

Boyle's face stiffened and he coughed awkwardly.

'Me, sir?' Jackson enquired, wholly oblivious.

'If you hadn't fallen and knocked the vase out of place, its location would have remained hidden – it's the perfect hiding space. Why, I doubt this heavy vase is ever moved, even when the cleaner comes in here.' Carson marvelled at the ingenuity of the lever's hiding place.

'I suppose you're right, sir,' Jackson said, smiling to himself.

'You got lucky, Jackson, but let's not get too carried away,' Boyle interjected, eager to remind the officer of his duty of care.

'Sorry, sir.'

'Anyway, let's not waste any more time, Jackson. Grab that lantern and lead the way.' Boyle replied.

As Jackson opened the panel further, they found themselves looking, not down a tunnel, as they had in the library but, rather startlingly, at an aged wooden ladder.

'I say! Now that's a turn up for the books!' Doctor Carson exclaimed, peering up the gaping hole that was now directly above them into a pit of darkness.

'I wasn't expecting that,' Boyle admitted, 'But needs must! Up you go, Jackson.'

Jackson moved towards the ladder, putting his first foot on the bottom rung. The old wooden step groaned as he lifted his full weight onto it, causing a nervous Jackson to back down.

'I don't know, sir, doesn't feel all that safe!'

'The absurdity of youth, eh, doctor! Stand aside then boy, it looks as if I will have to go first.'

With that, Inspector Boyle squeezed past Jackson and moved at once up onto the ladder. Again, the wood groaned under his weight, which was considerably more than the younger officer's and yet, it stood firm. Satisfied he wasn't going to come crashing back down, Boyle continued his ascent through the narrow vertical passageway and towards the glimmer of light high above.

When he was firmly out of sight, Carson called after him to check if he too could now ascend.

'Everything OK, Inspector? I am going to begin my climb now.'

'Very well, doctor, leave Jackson at the bottom though, as it's hardly a spacious room up here. Besides, we wouldn't want him to develop a fear of heights!'

Jackson grimaced at the sarcasm from his superior officer but remained happily planted at the entrance to the passage, secretly pleased that he wouldn't have to climb into the unknown space above. The excitement of the evening had been undeniable, but he would be lying if he didn't now find himself yearning for the relative peace of his desk back at the station house.

Doctor Carson, on the other hand, was thriving on the sense of intrigue that had encompassed the evening's activities. As he climbed the ladder into the darkness, he found his thoughts drifting back to Miss Lightwood and he made a mental note to thank her for the insightful tip-off that had led them here.

As he made his way to the top rung of the ladder, the light reached him and he pulled his way out of the steep vertical passage and into a small but neatly decorated snug, hidden high up in one of the old manor's tallest turrets.

The room, if you could call it that, consisted of a high back armchair and a small desk overlooking a tall thin window. Boyle was stood looking out of the window when his compatriot entered the room.

'Ah, there you are, doctor! Quite the surprise feature this, eh?!'

'Good lord, I have never seen such a place, what's the meaning of it all?'

'That's what we need to find out. This old narrow slit window reminds me of some sort of medieval fortress where a bowman would target his unsuspecting enemy from up high,' Boyle chuckled.

'Do you suppose this room has always been like

this?'

'Oh no, I wouldn't have thought so! I suspect this once served no greater purpose then to hoist a flag atop the manor flagpole.'

'There WAS a flagpole once upon a time. I remember Lord Avery telling me about it during one of my bedside vigils with him,' Doctor Carson exclaimed.

'Oh, really? Any idea what happened to it? As far as I can recollect, I've never seen one here before.

'Quite so, Inspector! Apparently, the pole was hit by lightning during a great storm around the turn of the century and Lord Avery's father had it removed through fear it could set the whole place alight.'

'Not an altogether stupid idea then!' Boyle mused, moving to the aged high back armchair which sat awkwardly in the centre of the circular room and just a few feet away from the impending doom of the open hole to the passageway.

'But it doesn't explain how a small writing desk and this armchair came to be up here now does it, doctor.'

'No, it certainly does not. I would fancy it was quite the feat getting them up here through that narrow vertical hole. How on earth do you think they managed it?!'

Boyle scanned the room once more and then a wry smile appeared across his face.

'The 'how' isn't the question, dear Doctor Carson! Why, see there?! That old hook on the ceiling beam looks like a ship's pulley used for loading cargo'.

'By jove, you're right!'

'I suspect they simply harnessed the furniture and pulled it up here with that. A tricky, labour intensive exercise, yes, but perfectly doable with the right equipment! No, the real questions we are left with is by WHOM was this done and WHY.'

Doctor Carson was inclined to agree with the Inspector. It seemed an utterly thankless task to bring this furniture up here into this small snug. There were plenty of grand rooms downstairs with amazing views of the grounds beyond, so what was the need for this rather cramped viewing portal?

'Perhaps the desk holds a clue?' he uttered, more in hope than anything as Inspector Boyle began the process of searching the small wooden desk's only compartment.

'Aha! Doctor you really ought to consider that career change!' Boyle chuckled heartily, pulling a photo frame from the drawer.

'Does that mean you've found something?!'

'I would say so – look!' Boyle smirked, handing over the photo frame.

The photo frame was small, made of ivory with intricate detailing. The picture it held was an old sepia portrait of a beautiful young woman with dark curly hair. Her eyes were most striking, glistening back at the doctor with an intensity he had seldom seen before.

'I say! What a beautiful woman - but who do you suppose it is?'

'That's just the thing, doctor. I don't know! But one thing I AM sure of, is that it is not Lady Avery.'

'Yes, you're right about that – I've seen many a picture of Lady Avery in her youth and while she was a very beautiful woman in her own right, this girl is utterly striking.'

'This mystery just seems to grow with every discovery we make,' Boyle uttered, pulling his small notebook from his pocket and scribbling yet more notes.

Doctor Carson continued to observe the photo and the frame. As he ran his hand over the frame, he noted a distinct anomaly on the back of it and turning it over, discovered why.

'Inspector! There's an inscription on this!'

Boyle immediately joined the doctor and read the small inscription on the underside of the frame.

'Dearest William, ever yours Daphne.'

'Daphne? Does that name ring any bells with you, doctor? Anybody on your rounds with such a name?'

'Why, no, it doesn't, I'm afraid. A childhood sweetheart, perhaps?'

'Quite possibly, yes. It does seem curious why he would keep it so long and hidden away up here though.'

'Yes, not the sort of behaviour I would expect from a sane man, especially one of the calibre of Lord Avery.'

Boyle continued to inspect the desk, which on most parts seemed to be full of old, hand scrawled notes. Pulling the notes out, he read as Doctor Carson decided to inspect the chair. The old leather wingback was cracked and creased from years of use, but seemingly possessed none of the secrets they were becoming accustomed to in other areas of the house.

'Doctor, I think I may have found something which could very well throw this case wide open,' Boyle chirped up, delight in his voice.

'Really? What is it?'

'It's a letter from the mysterious Daphne to Lord Avery dated 40 years ago – take a read.'

Doctor Carson took the letter and held it in his hands in the dim light of the room. The stained yellow handwritten note showcased the delicate hand of the striking young woman.

October 9th 1890

Dearest William

How long it feels since I last held you in my arms!

It's such a cruel fate that separates us by such a great distance, and I long for your safe return to Oakford and to me. I wonder what you are having to do in such distant foreign lands. This war you're fighting is something I cannot fathom – why our men are needed in such an uncivilised place is something I am yet to comprehend.

Oakford is ghastly silent without you here; I can scarcely walk around the village without believing I see your shadow, and how I wish it would be you. Darling, I love you so very greatly and I cannot wait for your return.

To become your wife, Mrs Avery, will be the greatest honour of my life and I'm counting the days until we can finally be together properly. My Dearest, I must tell you something which I only hope brings joy to you the way it has to me. I am with child William, your child, and I intend to have our baby as I know would be your blessing. Mother is sending me to stay with my great aunt in Hertfordshire to avoid scandal, but I know when we marry, I can return, and we can live together as a happy family in Oakford.

I am sorry this will come as a tremendous shock to you when you are so far from home, but please know I will be waiting for you when you return. Your father refuses me at Oakford Court and wanted me to give up the child, but I will not. I hope you agree with my decision and I wait with great anticipation for your return.

Ever yours my darling with all my heart,

Daphne

When Doctor Carson had finished the letter, he was momentarily stunned. The sheer idea that Lord Avery would have an illegitimate child baffled him.

'Quite the turn up, eh, doctor.'

'I am lost for words,' he replied breathlessly.

'We must handle this information sensitively. At no point has there been any indication this child was acknowledged by Lord Avery as far as I can tell, and the fact this is hidden up here suggests it is something perhaps even Lady Avery is unaware of.'

'You mean to say Lord Avery kept secret an illegitimate child for nearly 40 years of his life?! I struggle to believe such an honourable man could do such a thing.'

'I am not sure what it means yet, doctor. But if

there is a secret child, then that raises the possibility there is also another heir with a claim to Oakford Court. Suppose they found out upon Lord Avery's passing that they had a birth right to the estate – I would say that's pretty compelling grounds for motive, wouldn't you?'

'Well, I suppose that is entirely plausible, Inspector! But why wait all these years to stake your claim? Surely it would have been easier to do so whilst Lord Avery was still alive?'

Inspector Boyle pondered the question at length, gazing out of the slit window onto the dark grounds beyond.

'Perhaps they didn't find out about their connection to Lord Avery until after his death? It is possible, is it not? All the papers would have reported on it and this Daphne, or a relative, could easily have let slip after so many years?'

'If that is so, Inspector, then this mystery is only going to get even more complicated than it already was!' Doctor Carson cursed. 'Worst still, we still haven't found the murder weapon!'

'Yes, that is frustrating doctor, but I suspect that this information could prove just as invaluable in our investigations.'

The two men stood a moment longer in silence in the confined space, before Carson asked one more question.

'Do we tell Lady Avery or anyone about this?'

'No, I think we should tread carefully. It is a delicate subject, and we need to investigate it first – try and discover who knows what about this before we cause any potential distress.'

Doctor Carson nodded and moved over towards the ladder, to begin his descent. Inspector Boyle pocketed the letter and the photo frame and followed him down the ladder, each man treading into the darkness with care.

Jackson, who had spent the last ten minutes walking aimlessly around the master's study, was alerted to their descent by the noise of the creaking steps and jumped to attention at the entrance to the secret passageway.

'Any luck up there, sir?' Jackson asked Doctor Carson when he re-emerged at the bottom of the ladder.

Carson, cautious following the conversation with the Inspector, avoided the young man's gaze and replied meekly: 'Oh yes, Jackson, we found a snug up there – very unorthodox.'

The discovery of a snug was hardly a revelation in the eyes of the young officer, and he pressed further.

'A snug, sir? That seems rather odd to be hidden away with such care. Was there anyth...'

Before he could finish, Boyle appeared at the

bottom of the ladder and interrupted him.

'The murder weapon wasn't up there, boy, that's all you need to know for now. Our main goal tonight was to locate it and we have failed thus far.'

'Sorry to hear that, sir. What do we do next?'

Inspector Boyle had been asking himself that very question on his decent from the hidden snug. As perceptive as he was at unearthing answers to hidden mysteries, he had to confess he hadn't seen this revelation coming. Much like the young officer, he had expected the main discovery coming their way would have been locating the murder weapon, and yet that remained very much up in the air.

'I will go and meet with Lady Avery as requested, doctor. Perhaps you could join me? Jackson, I would say that we've done all we can here tonight, so you can head home and get some rest. Tomorrow could prove to be a very busy day indeed.'

The young officer wasn't about to argue. He had been on duty for nearly 12 hours now and the prospect of returning home to a warm bed had an appeal far greater than his current intrigue.

'If you're sure, sir? Thank you, sir.'

As the trio made their way back down the grand staircase and into the lobby of the house, Jackson turned for the front door.

'Good night, doctor.'

'Good night, Jackson. Thank you for all the assistance. I will be singing your praises next time I see your mother.'

'Thank you, sir,' the young officer blushed.

'Jackson, don't get too comfortable at home. We will be back here tomorrow at the earliest opportunity. That weapon is still on these grounds, I am sure of it, so we will search every inch of the estate until we locate it.' Boyle instructed.

'I look forward to it, sir,' Jackson replied drolly.

Jackson nodded his head at the two men and left the house. Hastening his departure down the driveway, he was keen to be long out of sight before the Inspector changed his mind and opted to keep them searching throughout the night.

The thought made him chuckle to himself but only slightly. In truth, he wouldn't put the notion past the Inspector. Boyle was nothing if not a perfectionist who seemed to thrive on the complexity of murder. Sleep, Jackson thought, held little esteem with the Inspector whilst he was on a case.

CHAPTER TWENTY SEVEN

It's cruel, but necessary

Dinner service was in full flow by the time the two intrepid explorers had finished traipsing through the secret passageways, and thus they had time alone to conjure up their next moves before meeting Lady Avery. They opted to wait in the library, and Inspector Boyle rung the service bell to alert Harley to their return.

'Doctor, we must approach the conversation with Lady Avery with great caution. I will try to lead the discussion in such a way that allows us to ascertain how much, if anything, she knows about Lord Avery's past.'

'I will follow your lead, Inspector, but we are basing all of this on a 40-year-old letter. Who's to know for certain this Daphne ever had a child?'

'We cannot be certain until we have a chance to review the birth records from that period, but for now any information we can get, to understand how much Lady Avery knows, will be crucial.'

Just then, they heard the door opening and in came Harley.

'You rang, sir. I trust you found the passageway you were looking for?' the old butler asked, his tone in no way indicating whether he was interested in the response or not.

'Thank you, Harley. We did indeed find it, but alas, it revealed nothing more than our previous excursions down here.'

Something flashed across Harley's face, the slightest reaction but nevertheless a noticeable and significant one which Boyle noted with great intrigue. It was a reaction of surprise.

'I am sorry to hear that, sir,' Harley replied, his composure regained.

Inspector Boyle nodded but quietly noted to himself his suspicion that Harley, was in fact, quite pleased by the lack of any findings.

'Yes, it was a shame. Thank you for your help

though, Harley, and if you can let Lady Avery know we are available at her convenience... we will wait here.'

'Very good, sir.'

When he had left to pass on their message, Inspector Boyle spoke up once more.

'Suppose Lady Avery did know about the illegitimate heir – wouldn't she have said something when we first interviewed her? It could very well lead to her son's murderer being revealed, after all? I see no reason why she would conceal it?'

'Yes, I quite agree with that. I believe it more likely she is oblivious to the existence of another child and considering the recent heartbreak she has endured; it would be cruel to inflict more.' Carson reasoned.

'Cruel, yes, but necessary, if it helps to solve this murder. It is something we have a duty to perform,' Boyle warned.

Doctor Carson reluctantly agreed, knowing they had little choice but to reveal the deceased lord's family 'skeletons', if it meant finding the killer. As they waited patiently for Lady Avery's arrival, both men sat in silence, alone with their thoughts.

The large wooden door eventually swung open, waking both from their deep thoughts as Harley stood aside, allowing Lady Avery to enter the room.

'Gentleman, thank you for waiting,' she said, extending her hand to Doctor Carson and then Inspector Boyle.

'Thank you for allowing us to access the house at this hour, your ladyship,' Boyle replied bowing his head.

'Not at all. I understand you have been searching for something in the tunnels?! Please, do sit.'

Both men duly obliged and sat on side-by-side high back chairs opposite the small sofa where Lady Avery had perched herself.

'Can I offer either of you a drink?' she continued.

'Certainly! But please allow me,' Doctor Carson offered, sensing an opportunity to step aside and allow Inspector Boyle to begin his interview.

'Thank you, doctor, I will have a sherry.'

'Of course, Lady Avery, and for you, Inspector? Perhaps you'll join me for a brandy?'

'Yes, why not.'

Carson stood and made his way over to the drinks trolley, taking his time to pour each order into the three crystal tumblers so as to allow Boyle to continue.

'In answer to your question, Lady Avery, yes we

had reason to investigate the hidden passageways as they were not known to us during the initial hunt for the murder weapon.'

'I shouldn't be surprised they hadn't been discussed originally; it has been over 30 years since they were even opened, to my knowledge,' Lady Avery mused.

'Yes, quite so, but nevertheless we had a duty to search them and we have now completed this part of our investigation.'

'It is very thorough of you, Inspector! I applaud your efforts.' Lady Avery exclaimed, 'And...'

'And what, Lady Avery?'

'Well, did you locate the murder weapon?'

'Oh, right, no I am afraid to say that is yet to be unearthed, but please rest assured we will continue our investigations at length in pursuit of it.'

'I have no doubts that you will, Inspector.'

'Were you aware of a passageway leading off from your husband's study, ma'am?' Boyle asked nonchalantly, as Doctor Carson brought over the drinks.

'I have heard one exists, yes,' she replied, stiffening slightly.

Carson handed her the sherry and she sipped it gratefully. 'Thank you, Doctor Carson.'

Inspector Boyle took his brandy and took a swig, before continuing his questions.

'So, to be clear, Lady Avery, you were aware of the passage but hadn't ever been in it personally.'

'I have not, Inspector, no. Can I ask if there is any relevance to this?'

'Sorry, Lady Avery, I am just obliged to outline our findings at this time. I am simply trying to paint a picture of the house and its occupants in order to better understand the layout. These tunnels have been a most unusual find for me! Were they common knowledge when you first met Lord Avery?'

'A rather odd question, Inspector, but, yes, I believe so. Although it was nearly 40 years ago and my memory isn't what it used to be!' she chuckled, sipping her drink once more.

'Yes, I suppose it was!' Boyle agreed chuckling 'It must have been quite different in Oakford back then.'

'Well, in many ways, yes, simpler perhaps! But, all things considered, not much ever changes around here.'

'Quite charming really. I think an old distant aunt of mine grew up around here,' Boyle continued.

'Oh, really Inspector?'

'Perhaps you've heard of her Lady Avery? Her name was Daphne.'

Inspector Boyle straightened in his chair and kept his eyes firmly poised on Lady Avery's reaction, looking for the slightest sign of recognition.

She replied without so much of a twitch. 'Daphne, you say? I can't recall having met a Daphne from Oakford, I'm afraid.'

'Ah, never mind! Perhaps I am getting confused with another village. He brushed off that line of enquiry and quickly changed tact. 'Did Lord Avery spend much time in his study, do you recall?'

'He would often retire for an evening of reading or writing, Inspector, as I have no doubt most men do. Even Mrs Boyle must be used to that?!'

Boyle chuckled, keen to keep the matriarchal lady on side. 'Why, yes, quite so! I believe that is all from me, Lady Avery, thank you. Doctor, do you have anything to add?'

'No, I don't believe I do at this time, Inspector. Lady Avery thank you for your time, and please be assured we will do everything in our power to bring your son's killer to justice.'

She smiled warmly at the doctor, her tough exterior softening just ever so slightly.

'Thank you, doctor, I have every faith in you

both and please continue to use Oakford Court as you see fit.'

The three of them chatted merrily from there, the strain of questioning lifted and attentions moving, as they often did in British tradition, to talk of the weather and gardening.

CHAPTER TWENTY EIGHT

The fountain

'You've had no luck finding the murder weapon then, I suppose?' Miss Morris enquired, sipping her tea as she sat in the bay window of the drawing room.

'I am afraid not, Miss Morris,' Doctor Carson replied.

'Oh, doctor, call me Lillie, please!'

'Yes, of course, sorry.' His face reddened slightly.

Lillie Morris enjoyed seeing the older man squirm in his seat. He was quite the typical British gentleman and she enjoyed his strait-laced approach.

'It is strange, though, is it not? The weapon just disappearing like that,' she continued.

'Strange indeed. I confess it has been perhaps the most frustrating part of this whole investigation! I am confident that finding the weapon will help solve the case.'

'Oh, I do hope this nightmare can end soon for everyone's sake. Poor Aunt Ellen is doing so superbly, but the strain must be unbearable. And, then there's mother! She is insufferable, desperately eager to return to Fowey.'

'Are you not keen to go home too?'

She pondered the answer for a moment as she carefully held on to her cup.

'To tell the truth, I am rather dreading going back.'

'Oh??' Carson raised an eyebrow in surprise. It had been the answer he had hoped for, but nevertheless it was unexpected.

'Please don't misunderstand me, doctor! It isn't that I dislike Fowey, far from it. I have had a good childhood there even since the tragedy of my father's passing! It's just....'

'Yes?'

'Oh, I don't know, it's just, I feel so happy here in Oakford. I like being around the people here.'

Doctor Carson held her gaze a moment longer

than he had anticipated, lost in a hopeful thought process.

'Doctor?' she queried, looking back concerned.

'Eh? Oh, sorry! I... I was rather distracted for a moment there,' he blushed once more.

Lillie Morris giggled, unsure where to look herself, before tactfully changing the subject to spare both of their blushes.

'Have you given up all hope of finding the murder weapon?'

'No, not at all! I am more determined than ever that we simply must find it! I honestly thought the tunnels held the answer. It all seemed to fit most superbly.'

'Tunnels?'

Doctor Carson cursed his loose tongue. The tunnels were on a need-to-know basis, Inspector Boyle had instructed him in no uncertain terms, and here he was running his mouth off so openly.

'I shouldn't have said anything! Please forget I mentioned that.'

'Forget? How can I possibly forget! Tunnels? Here at Oakford? How delightfully thrilling!'

'It isn't something that's well-known Miss M... Lillie.'

'Oh, don't worry, dear, you're safe with me! But

you simply must tell me about these tunnels? I always wondered if this old house held secrets!' She grasped his hand warmly.

The touch of her delicate hand on his eased his initial worries, and he found himself incapable of disappointing her.

'Alright, I'll bring you up to speed with the investigation, but promise me it will remain between us?'

'Mum's the word!' She crossed her lips to emphasise her silence.

'I recently discovered from one of my older patients that there had previously been small tunnels built here as secret passageways during the Great War. Naturally, this provided a part of the house we hadn't investigated during our initial searches for the murder weapon and, as such, we endeavoured to locate and explore the passageways.'

'And you found them?!' the excitement was palpable, as she leaned forward in her chair.

'Well, yes we did! But there was nothing really of note and certainly no murder weapon,' Carson replied quickly, eager to reduce down the detail he shared.

'That IS a shame! I can certainly understand why you'd see them as an ideal hiding place.'

'Yes, quite! I must confess I really thought one of

the tunnels would hold the answer.'

'Do tell me where these tunnels are? I should love to know, and, surely, there is no harm in me knowing if they hold nothing of interest at all?'

Doctor Carson pondered the reasoning of the young woman for a moment. He knew he had already compromised their investigation by taking her into his confidence, and yet he knew he couldn't bare the idea of disappointing her. He made the best decision he could.

'Alright, I suppose I can trust you. There are two tunnels, one was in the library and the other is in this very room.' He had wisely opted to avoid including the master's study and its tucked away private tower room.

'Oh, how exciting! One in here you say!? Where is it?'

'It's behind the fireplace over there,' he indicated.

'Do you suppose I can see it?!' she asked, almost giddy with excitement.

'I shouldn't see any harm in it, but there is not much to see with this one.'

They walked over to the fireplace and Doctor Carson preceded to press hard against the ornate figurine on the left-hand side. As before, the figure shifted and caused the hidden passageway to reveal itself.

'It's like something out of a novel!' Lillie Morris squealed in delight, as she cautiously peered into the dark void.

'You can go inside, but there isn't much room in this one – more of a small cupboard than anything else! Harley reckons it once held a whisky collection.'

'Oh, I don't need to, but I should have guessed Harley knew about these tunnels! He was most likely present when they were built!'

They both laughed as they came away from the passage entrance and Doctor Carson pushed the fireplace back to its normal place.

'The one in the library is more of a tunnel, but rather annoyingly it is blocked off halfway down.' Carson continued as they moved out of the drawing room and into the library.

'Blocked off? Do you suppose it went somewhere?'

'Apparently, it was intended to be an escape route out of the Court into the grounds during the war but was never completed because, thankfully, the war ended. See that red leather backed novel on the third shelf there? Pull it towards you.'

Lillie Morris followed the doctor's pointed finger and found the book. As she pulled it towards her, the large bookshelf came away from the wall and revealed the tunnel.

'Oh, how exciting! I feel just like a spy!' she said.

The two of them walked into the passageway and followed it until their progress was cut short by the dead end.

'And that's as far as the investigation took us.' Doctor Carson sighed, leaning on the solid stone wall that blocked their path.

Lillie Morris examined the wall carefully, running her hands down and along its cold surface with great interest. For several moments she didn't even look up, her attention so fixated on the wall.

'Is everything OK, Lillie?'

'Oh, yes, sorry! It's just….'

'What is it?'

'Never mind, I'm sure you'll think me a foolish little girl for even thinking it,' she smiled.

'I wouldn't ever think you foolish, Lillie,' Carson replied softly. 'Please tell me.'

'It's just rather odd, isn't it, that they would opt to dig this tunnel out from the house. I would have thought it easier to dig from both sides and meet in the middle? That way you can easily navigate to the right location. But it's a silly thought. There would be a noticeable entrance in the grounds and, as you said, they could have easily stopped the dig after the war before they even got as far as planning the other end.'

Doctor Carson pondered this theory in his mind. It hadn't dawned on him or any of the others that they might have dug the other end of the tunnel. They had hit a wall and accepted it, but interestingly Lillie had come across a more novel idea. Only a woman could think so logically, he mused to himself.

'Do you think I am foolish now?' Lillie enquired, her head hung low in embarrassment as she awaited any sort of response from the doctor.

'On the contrary, my dear. I think you are rather brilliant!' he beamed.

'Oh?'

'Why it's a marvellously simple idea and yet not one of us even contemplated it! You're right, it makes no sense whatsoever to simply dig blindly from the house. They must have known at least where they hoped to end up, and the best way to have known that would have been to mark it out and start digging both sides of the tunnel at the same time. Yes, you really are quite extraordinary, Lillie Morris!'

She blushed at the high praise but was also instantly relieved that her idea hadn't been ridiculed.

'Do you suppose that the other entrance might

still exist?'

'There's only one way to find out!' Doctor Carson replied buoyantly.

'How wonderfully exciting today is proving to be! Nothing like this ever found me in Fowey.'

❈ ❈ ❈

Having closed the bookcase doorway, the pair donned their overcoats and made their way out onto the landscaped grounds behind the house. It was late afternoon and the sun was slowly descending behind the great weeping willow which cornered the gravel path leading down to the lake. Despite the cold chill that remained in the air, the wind had mercifully died down, leaving Doctor Carson and Lillie Morris to continue their search for the other potential tunnel opening.

'Where do we even begin?' Lillie asked, her excitement waning by the sheer scale of the land in front of her.

'I think you were right in your assessment about the grounds/ It would have left a noticeable void which would have been seen by now,' Carson began, scanning the scene in front of them.

'Well, if we agree on that point, surely the tunnel must have come out either on the gravel path on via one of the outbuildings,' Lillie said, pointing in the direction of the garden sheds off to the right of the property, which bordered the walled garden.

'I suspect that the sheds would be too far away for the tunnel,' Carson observed.

'So, we are left with the path itself? The gravel could easily conceal a trap door.'

'Yes, it could, and then there is the fountain as well,' Carson mentioned casually, pointing towards the ornate fountain sitting in the middle of the grounds just beyond the terraced patio. Built at the same time as the original house, it depicted two curled mythical sea creatures bending towards the bowl of the fountain, their tails connecting together at the top where the water would usually sprout out during the warmer months.

'The fountain! Of course! How clever you are dear doctor,' Lillie squeezed his arm with appreciation. 'It must be there.'

He wasn't sure if it was logic that had brought him to the fountain, but he was certainly not in a hurry to correct the young woman's positivity, especially considering how impressed she had seemed by his observation.

They approached with anticipation, both scouring the fountain's circular concrete wall for any indication that it might conceal a hidden entranceway.

'It seems rather solid,' Carson said, the hope fading from his voice.

'But the cement seams which separate the sections of the fountain wall could easily conceal the opening! Don't lose hope just yet – who would have realised the fireplace could open!' The optimism in her voice was reassuring and Carson soon found himself closely examining the seams with a renewed vigour.

Once they had checked all the seams, it was impossible to be certain whether or not there was, in fact, a concealed entrance.

'What now?' Doctor Carson said out loud, more to himself than anyone in particular.

'We are looking for the wrong thing here,' Lillie interjected.

'What do you mean?'

'You said it yourself, doctor. The last two tunnels were so perfectly concealed that the only way to access them was to find the hidden lever! That's what we should be looking for, not the door itself but the access lever!'

Doctor Carson found himself once more awestruck by the brilliant practical mind alongside him. Women truly were a superior breed.

'Remarkable, truly remarkable,' he mused.

Again, Lillie felt her cheeks reddening at the compliment offered up in her direction.

The two of them began to probe the fountain's surround at length, hoping to find a loose slab which would move under their pressure. The circular base was utterly solid, and nothing seemed to budge even an inch, leaving their only alternative to be the two mythical sea creatures which curved elegantly above them.

'I can't even reach those,' Lillie said, stretching as best she could across the fountain's edge towards the central statuettes.

'I can, but not enough to apply the sort of pressure that was needed on the fireplace,' Doctor Carson stated as he climbed onto the edge of the circular surround and found his balance as he leaned in towards the two creatures.

'Oh, do please be careful, doctor. You will catch your death if you fall in that freezing water below the ice.'

For the second time in under a week, Doctor Carson contemplated the prospects of an icy dip in water but once more found his desire to find the murder weapon far outweighed his fears for his own safety. Leaning across, he managed to balance himself by applying his upper body weight to the solid statues in front of him.

'It would make sense if it were the left-hand sculpture, wouldn't you say? Judging by the fireplace!' As he said this, he turned his attention to the left sculpture. The sculpture didn't budge, despite his considerable efforts.

'Perhaps it is the right one? A sort of counter act to the internal entrance?' Lillie offered.

Carson moved onto the right-hand sculpture and, once again, applied as much pressure as he could. This time, however, the stone gave way slightly and retreated into the sculpture.

At once, a large portion of the circular wall creaked forward to reveal an entrance directly beneath the fountain.

'You did it!' Lillie squealed with palpable excitement as she forced open the entrance and peered down the newly revealed steep stone stairwell that led into a darkened passage.

'It was your idea to try the opposite sculpture that did it!' Carson replied, chivalrously, as he climbed down from the fountain and found himself alongside Lillie looking into the dark abyss below.

'Well, merely a process of elimination, but thank you. Should we go down?'

'I don't see why we shouldn't! We just ought to ensure we do not disturb anything that could be pivotal to the Inspector's case later on.'

'It's all so mysterious! Who would have thought that there was a tunnel, right here, all this time?! I must have played around this fountain for hours when I was younger!' she remembered.

Doctor Carson pulled out the torch he had brought from the house and stepped down the first step into a cold, damp passage under the fountain.

'Watch your step, Lillie. It is very slippery where the moisture has gotten onto the steps.'

As the two of them descended, the steps became darker and harder to navigate until, mercifully, they reached the flat ground of the concrete passage.

'This is the tunnel that leads up to the library.'

'I can't see how far it goes?' Lillie peered forward tentatively into the darkness and grabbed hold of the doctor's arm with a sense of trepidation.

'We must follow it and see if there is anything here.'

Carson was himself slightly anxious about what they might come across in such a dire spot underground, but steeled himself, nonetheless, buoyed by her confidence and enthusiam.

The tunnel really was nothing more than a concrete passage, but the lack of light and the damp smell, along with their active imaginations at what may be lurking in its depths, created an eerie atmosphere which put them both on edge.

Silently, they continued along the passageway for nearly 400 yards until the torch beam came across a blank wall directly in front of them. Lillie was the first to break the silence that had encompassed them.

'Look, doctor! That must be the wall which you found on the opposite side from the library.'

'Yes, that's the wall alright. Can you see anything else?'

He moved the torchlight around the perimeter of the wall as they moved ever closer to their destination. The beam reflected nothing more than concrete until landing abruptly onto a heap of cloth on the bottom right-hand side of the passage.

'I say! There's something down there.'

'Should we see what it is?' Lillie asked, the tension rising in her voice.

'We must,' he moved forward tentatively while Lillie stayed back. As it came into clearer view, he realised the cloth was, in fact, a pillowcase concealing something that itself was wrapped inside another pillowcase.

Doctor Carson was eager to ensure they didn't do anything that might tamper with potential evidence, but he had to know all the same if this was what they had been looking for ever since that fateful morning.

Moving the pillowcase aside gently with the handle of his torch, he peered in and saw the glint of a blade. A blade with an edge clearly covered in dried blood.

'What is it?' Lillie asked softly from the darkness behind him.

'I think we've found it, Lillie!' he replied, the excitement clear in his voice.

'You mean the murder weapon?!'

'Yes, it's definitely the missing weapon hidden in a pillowcase.'

'Oh, well that's wonderful news!' Lillie exclaimed, delighted. 'What do we do now?

Doctor Carson had been pondering the very same question as he stared down at the weapon. He knew there was only one thing they could do.

'I think you will have to go and find Inspector Boyle, Lillie.'

'Me? Why can't we both go? Surely we can pick it up if it's in the pillowcase.'

'Possibly, yes, but if we move it, we risk losing vital clues which a skilled eye may find. It's a risk we cannot take.'

'Yes, you're right,' Lillie sighed, 'but why can't we just leave it here and head back together?'

'The last time I took my eyes off this weapon it went missing and it has taken all this time to relocate it. I must stay in case the murderer has seen us and comes back for it.'

Lillie Morris felt quite faint at the thought of having to go back along the dark passageway alone, but that paled in comparison with the idea of leaving the doctor alone in the dark, a sitting duck if the murderer did, indeed, return.

'Oh, it's a wicked thought. I cannot bare the idea of leaving you in here all alone.'

'You must, be quick and get the Inspector – I'll be alright.'

'But what if the killer does return?!'

It was a thought Carson couldn't bring himself to consider unless he had to.

'Let's pray they don't, but I can look after myself,' he replied, the conviction in his voice less than certain.

Lillie wanted nothing more than to get out of this dark eerie space but, even so, was still reluctant to leave him behind.

'Please, Lillie, go now.' Carson repeated.

'I'll... I'll be as quick as I can, I promise.'

'I know you will. Here, take the torch,' he said, handing her the only remaining source of light.

Even in the now near total darkness of the tunnel, they both looked longingly for a moment before Lillie turned and hurried away down the passageway back to the fountain.

For a moment, Carson watched the light beam bouncing off the wall as she went before the darkness enveloped him and he was left in silence and just his own sense of dread.

CHAPTER TWENTY NINE

The weapon holds the clue

Inspector Boyle had arrived at Oakford Court less than fifteen minutes earlier and was in the process of inspecting the chauffeur's car by one of the outbuildings, when the sound of fast footsteps approaching across the gravel caught his attention.

The approaching figure was young Lillie Morris, looking decidedly anxious as she hurried over to him.

'Inspector!'

'Is everything alright, Miss Morris?'

'You must come with me straight away. It's the weapon,' she panted, desperately trying to catch her breath.

'The what?'

'The weapon! We've found it – Doctor Carson is with it now.'

'I say! Where?!' Boyle was seldom a man who found himself surprised, but this was quite a turn up for the books.

'In a secret tunnel under the fountain.'

'The fountain?! Most interesting! Lead the way Miss Morris,' Boyle continued before yelling, 'JACKSON!'

The young hapless policeman popped out of the staff entrance where he had been chatting happily to the young parlour maid, Doris.

'Yes, sir?'

'Follow me, boy.'

Jackson hurried after the Inspector and the two of them followed Miss Morris around the side of the large house and onto the back lawn, leading down to the fountain.

As they arrived at the location both men were startled to find the concrete wall of the fountain ajar, revealing the long stone staircase down into the darkness below.

'My god, it's another tunnel boss.' Jackson exclaimed.

Inspector Boyle gave a tired look at the young

man. 'Yes, thank you, Jackson, I had noticed.'

'Sorry, sir,' Jackson blushed, 'but I thought we had found all the tunnels!'

'It's the other end of the blocked tunnel you found in the library,' Lillie interjected.

'And how, Miss Morris, do you know about that?' Boyle enquired.

It was Lillie's turn to blush, but she also knew they were wasting time.

'Doctor Carson told me, in strict confidence, I might add! It doesn't matter now anyway; we found the tunnel and the weapon and now he is alone down there, and we must get to him.'

Boyle, whilst irked that the young woman had been taken into Doctor Carson's confidence, knew she was right.

'Jackson, take that torch and lead the way. Miss Morris, you stay up here.'

Lillie was quite happy with the arrangement and handed over the torch without another word. Jackson, somewhat less impressed with the plan, took it and reluctantly began his descent into the gloomy tunnel with Boyle close behind.

※ ※ ※

Sat alone in the pitch black, Doctor Carson was trying to remain calm whilst his mind raced with all sorts of bloody possibilities. His heroic plan to remain with the weapon had made total sense to him when they were both there with the torch and, yet, now alone in the dark, he was definitely regretting the decision. It had also dawned on him that he very easily could and should have followed Lillie up the tunnel and waited at the entrance. It was a dead end after all!

'Utter fool,' he muttered to himself.

He dared not leave now in-case someone was in the tunnel waiting for him. It was a preposterous thought he tried to tell himself and, yet, his mind couldn't help but drift back to it at every opportunity.

There was nothing he could do but sit and wait. The minutes had passed painstakingly slowly. Each passing second had felt like an hour in the pitch-black room. His hand remained rested on the pillowcase, guarding his prize, whilst his ears were alert, ready for the slightest indication of noise.

How have I got to this point? he pondered as he sat on the cold stone floor. As a general practitioner in a small rural community, death was part and parcel of his life and yet it had never been thrust so dramatically into his path. The murder of Gerald Avery had certainly been an utter shock to his system, and yet, he had to confess the subsequent hunt for the murderer had made him feel more alive than he had felt in some time. Then there was Lillie Morris. Her appearance into his life had awoken feelings that had remained suppressed for many years, feeling of unfailing love, he began to realise. It had dawned on him that what he was truly missing in his life was someone to share it with, but he couldn't begin to imagine where to start, until now.

'You just tell her how you feel man,' he said to himself out loud.

Just then, he thought he had heard a noise some way down the tunnel. Instantly, he froze and pricked his ears to the darkness, adamant he had heard footsteps.

For a moment nothing but the still air surrounded him, and he began to wonder he was going mad.

'Pull yourself together, Carson,' he sighed.

A moment later, though, he was certain he could hear footsteps and they were dangerously close. Panic began to set in as his mind raced. It must be Lillie with the Inspector, he tried to reassure himself, but what if it wasn't? Was he really prepared to come face-to-face with the murderer, all alone in a dark hole like this?

'Doctor?!' the familiar voice of Inspector Boyle greeted him, as the beam from a torch rounded the last bend towards his location.

A great sense of relief rushed through him as he heard his friend's voice. He cursed his own paranoia as he saw the outline of the two policemen appear from the darkness.

'Am I glad to see you, Inspector!'

'I bet you are – utter madness staying down here in the dark, dear boy,' Boyle chuckled as he helped Doctor Carson to his feet.

'It was rather! Seemed the right thing to do at the time. But at least we have the weapon!'

'You're sure it's the same one you saw in the room?' Boyle's voice became more serious.

'Well, it is dark but, yes, I'm certain. The ornate handle carvings are the same and it has bloodstains on the blade.'

'Didn't I say we'd make a detective out of you, doctor? You could learn a thing or two from the doctor here, Jackson.'

'Yes, sir...' Jackson sighed.

'Oh, I'm not sure about all that,' Carson blushed 'It was really Lillie who led me here.... where is she by the way?'

'We left Miss Morris at the top by the fountain. Now, I will inspect the site and check it is safe to remove the weapon.'

Inspector Boyle moved closer to where the pillowcase was laying in the corner and instructed Jackson to hold the light over him. It was immediately obvious that the weapon had been wrapped in one pillowcase, then carried in another out to the tunnel, where it had been left in the furthest possible corner to avoid detection. Boyle's experience of crime scenes told him there was little harm in moving the weapon back to the surface to inspect it more closely as, if there were clues to be found, they were most likely IN the pillowcase rather than around it. He spent a few more moments carefully looking over the pillowcase and the surrounding area before he was satisfied with his conclusions.

'Jackson, put on a pair of gloves and bring that pillowcase out with you, and be careful not to knock anything on the way.'

'Right you are, sir,' the young officer duly removed his gloves from his coat pocket, put them on and gingerly picked up the pillowcase.

The three of them made their way back along the tunnel in near silence, each one deep in thought at what this significant discovery could mean to the investigation. It was only once they began to see the light seeping in from above did Boyle speak once more.

'When we get out of here, we will go at once

to the library and review the evidence. Jackson, you are to find Harley and instruct that we aren't to be disturbed. Do not tell him why at this moment in time.'

'Yes, sir.'

'Doctor, you and Miss Morris will join me in the library to discuss what all this means.'

'Yes, of course, Inspector. I'll just be glad to be back at ground level.'

As they climbed out from the tunnel one-by-one, led by Doctor Carson, Lillie was waiting with an anxious look on her face as she sat to the side of the entrance.

When she caught sight of Doctor Carson emerging from the passage she rose immediately to her feet, relief rushing over her as she embraced him affectionately.

'Oh, thank goodness you're alright. I was so scared!'

The warmth of her body pressed against him and the concern in her voice made it all worthwhile for Doctor Carson, and for a moment he allowed himself to hug her back.

'It's all OK, Lillie – we've done it!'

Inspector Boyle was next to emerge and seeing the embracing couple, he coughed awkwardly, causing them both to pull away sheepishly.

Once Jackson had come up safely with the pillowcase and weapon in hand, Boyle and Doctor Carson pushed the stone entrance back into its normal position and the four of them stood with the fountain towering over them, unassuming and calm in the afternoon's winter sun.

'Right then, let's go and inspect this weapon and see if we can find ourselves a killer,' Boyle rubbed his hands. The glint in his eye that Carson had seen time and time again was back and shining brighter than ever. The hunt was truly on.

✽ ✽ ✽

Once they had made their way safely back to the library, Boyle sent Jackson off to find Harley and closed the large wooden doors behind him. Confident they wouldn't be disturbed, he put on his own pair of gloves and removed the covered weapon from the first pillowcase, which he laid flat on the top of a small coffee table ready for inspection.

Doctor Carson and Lillie stood back and watched quietly as Boyle examined the pillowcase for any sign of fingerprints or hairs.

'I think it's safe to say there isn't anything of note to be found on this one. It would have been taken from the fresh linen. Now, let's look at the weapon.'

As he slowly unwrapped the weapon from the pillowcase and carefully laid it out on the table, Lillie gasped at the sight of the dried blood on the blade.

'The handle is certainly unusual,' Boyle commented as he observed the ornately carved ivory handle.

'Yes, I thought as much when I first saw it. Mckelvie rather fancied it was of Indian origins,' Carson replied.

'Indian? That's most interesting. Have either of you seen this weapon or any like it in this house before?'

Both pondered the question for a moment before Doctor Carson replied: 'No, I've never seen a weapon like this before, but the pattern is familiar.'

'Oh, yes?'

'I am certain I've seen this pattern on one of the trinkets Lord Avery or the Colonel brought back from the colonies,' Lillie recalled.

'Does that mean Lord Avery may have been killed by one of his own souvenirs?' Doctor Carson queried.

Inspector Boyle frowned; the idea didn't sit well with him. His men had thoroughly searched the property, and nothing seemed amiss.

'I am not sure about that, doctor – but if this weapon does link back to the colonies it certainly provides an interesting connection to several of our suspects.'

'Yes, I dare say it does. So, we aren't any closer to the truth?!' Carson realised, dejected.

'Possibly not, but that's not to say we can't use this discovery to our advantage.'

'How do you propose we do that?'

'Perhaps, Miss Morris, you would be so kind as to go and find your uncle for us and ask him if he will join us for a while.'

'I don't follow,' Doctor Carson replied.

'I think I do,' Miss Morris smiled. 'I will fetch him at once, Inspector.'

With that, she left the room at an enthusiastic pace, leaving the two men alone with the weapon.

'You are right, doctor. A very bright young woman that one!'

'Yes, quite so,' he said, allowing his thoughts to trail off for a moment before continuing, 'but what's the meaning of getting the Colonel?'

'I rather fancy he can help us shed some light on this weapon's origins which, in turn, could lead us to our killer.'

'Quite! But…but what if he is involved?' Doctor Carson enquired tentatively, even though he highly doubted it was the Colonel. However, the event of the past few days had taught him to remain wary of virtually everyone.

'Well, I suppose his reaction to seeing the dagger will go a long way to confirming or disproving his innocence,' Boyle smiled to himself. 'But for now, we must clean the blood off the dagger before they return.'

Using water from the drinks trolley and the remaining pillowcase, he scrubbed off the dry blood and stuffed the pillowcase behind the chair.

'Isn't that tampering with the evidence, Inspector?' Doctor Carson gasped as he watched on.

'There is nothing else we can glean from this, but I wouldn't want the Colonel, if he is innocent, to know it's the murder weapon – not just yet.'

'Really?'

'You'll have to trust me on this, doctor. I have a theory in mind,' Boyle replied, the glint in his eyes indicating his cognitive process was far more advanced than the good doctor's.

CHAPTER THIRTY

An experience in New Guinea

A few minutes passed before a knock on the door was followed by Miss Morris returning with her uncle, Colonel Avery. 'Ah. Colonel, thank you for joining us!' said Boyle, expressing his genuine gratitude.

'Not at all, Inspector. My niece tells me you'd like some advice on colonial artefacts?' he enquired, the look on his face suggesting he took great pride in being summoned for his expertise on the matter.

'In a way, I would, yes,' Boyle replied amicably, directing the Colonel to take a seat in one of the high back chairs.

'Can I get you a drink, Colonel?' Doctor Carson

offered.

'No, thank you, doctor! I'd rather not drink till the evening – keep your lot at bay!' he replied with a hint of humour, although his tone suggested he was entirely serious.

'Very well then,' Boyle interrupted. 'Colonel, you have spent plenty of time on the continent during your military career, correct?'

The mention of his military past instantly energised the Colonel, who immediately sat to attention in his seat. 'That is correct, sir! I have been to every corner of the globe! Why, there was even a time my platoon came face-to-face with a tribe of cannibals in New Guinea, now that was an experience!'

Admittedly, whilst the idea of how the Colonel and his regiment had managed to escape a tribe of cannibals was extremely intriguing to Inspector Boyle, he nonetheless decided it was best to stop the Colonel's story in its tracks and get back to the job at hand.

'Fascinating! But I was rather hoping you might be able to take a look at one of the weapons we have found in the house and let me know of its origins? I imagine it's African, but you see I've had a wager with the good doctor, and he seems to think it's of Asian descent!'

Doctor Carson was unaware of their 'bet' but

played along, dutifully nodding enthusiastically.

Inspector Boyle pulled the weapon from its concealed place alongside his chair and placed it on the table in front of the Colonel. He watched both the Colonel's expression and that of Miss Morris. If the latter was surprised to see the weapon without its bloodstained apperance, she concealed the fact impressively and played her part effortlessly.

Colonel Avery didn't look surprised or worried to see the weapon, but he was certainly baffled by it.

'Well, that is an unusual one! You say you found it here in the house?'

'Oh yes, up in Lord Avery's study – just became of interest to us for a friendly wager as it seemed so different to the rest of his collection!' Boyle stated as he tried to offset any suspicions from the elder man.

'It is not one I've seen here before, but I'm afraid to say you;re both off the pace, as it were – this is an Indian tribal blade,' Colonel Avery declared, holding the weapon in his hands as he examined its ornate handle.

'Indian?! You are sure of that, Colonel?' Doctor Carson exclaimed.

The Colonel gave the doctor an annoyed glance.

'Of course I'm sure, saw plenty like this over there!'

'Yes, quite so,' Carson retreated, keen not to offend him further.

'Well, that's a dead rubber then, doctor.' Boyle laughed to himself, keen to continue the conversation. 'Thank you, Colonel, it really is a beautiful piece, and you say you've never seen it here before?'

'No! My brother has a vast collection, but he wasn't in India during his military career, so it's rather odd! Must be a souvenir gifted to him,' he replied casually.

'I'm sure you're right, Colonel! Now you must tell us about that experience in New Guinea.'

Inspector Boyle settled into his chair and listened as the Colonel began his rather vivid recollection to the group. Despite the story's rather far-fetched narrative, Boyle's mind began to wander back to the facts of the case and, finally, he felt the jigsaw puzzle pieces were beginning to align.

Tomorrow, he felt, would be a very significant day. For, if his hunch was right, and it had seldom been wrong, tomorrow would be the day he revealed the identity of the murderer.

CHAPTER THIRTY ONE

The killer is revealed

Following the Colonel's insightful examination of the weapon, and his colourful trip down memory lane, Inspector Boyle had made his excuses and left the house in a hurry.

He spent the rest of the afternoon following up on his hunch and had informed Doctor Carson to arrange for the house party to be present the following afternoon for an important update on their investigation.

He then called Mr Mckelvie and, after a lengthy discussion, it was determined that he would travel down from London once more and be present for the gathering with the rest of the group.

The next morning, Mr Mckelvie met Inspector Boyle at the police station and the two remained locked in deep conversation for some hours before making their way to Oakford Court to meet with the rest of the ensemble.

The last time they had all been sat in the drawing room of Oakford Court like this was the morning after Gerald Avery's murder. Inspector Boyle had cast a critical eye over each of them then, trying to understand who had the motive to kill poor Gerald. Now, he knew exactly who the murderer was within their midst and the anticipation in the room was electric.

'Ladies and gentlemen, thank you for joining us again today.'

'Well, we hardly had much of a choice in the matter!' the Colonel grumbled.

'I assure you, Colonel, it is absolutely imperative that you are all present. For, you see, amongst us today is the murderer of Mr Gerald Avery.'

Audible gasps of shock swirled around the room. Even the usually stoic Harley looked altogether shaken.

'Now, that is a turn up for the books!' Richard Haymer exclaimed. 'Suppose you'll pin it on me? The last remaining heir in a fit of rage, isn't that how those old detective stories always go!' he suggested, although no one else found the comment even the slightest bit amusing.

Inspector Boyle scanned the room theatrically as he replied: 'Actually, Mr Richard Haymer is not the murderer.'

'You can't seriously think any one of us is a cold-hearted killer?' Mrs Langtry blurted out, more out of nervousness than anything.

'Oh, but it is a fact, I'm afraid, Mrs Langtry! Since the beginning of my investigation, there has been a clear stumbling block that has continued to trouble me. It is the killer's motive. When Doctor Carson and I interviewed each of you, we established two critical factors. One was where each of you were on the night leading up to Gerald Avery's untimely death. And the other, was whether any of you had a motive for his murder. Without one, we knew we wouldn't find our killer. Normally, it is simply a process of elimination, identifying the suspect with the most evident motive. But, in this case, it has been much trickier because it very soon became clear that each of you had a motive for the killing.' He glanced at the startled expressions facing him.

'What possible motive could I have had for killing my own nephew?!' Mrs Langtry shrieked once again.

'OK, ma'am, let's start with you. We learnt you eloped at a young age with an older man, an artist no less! The marriage was one that didn't sit well with your brothers and you found yourself an outcast from the rest of the family circle. Yes, you had a yearly allowance following your husband's untimely death, but resentment set in, didn't it, Mrs Langtry?! Not only did your family do nothing to support your artist husband's failing career, but you also blame them for his death don't you.'

'This is utter nonsense! Why on earth would I blame my family for a boating accident?' she replied, flustered.

'Because there was NO boating accident, Mrs Langtry, was there! Your husband drowned himself as he couldn't cope with his failing career.'

More gasps escaped from those around the room. Mrs Langtry rose from her seat, anger on her face and tears in her eyes.

'That's enough, Inspector! I won't sit here and listen to your lies.'

'Oh, just stop it, mother!' Lillie shouted at her startled stepmother. 'Stop it. You're lying to yourself! You always have. Papa did drown himself; I've always known it and yet, you refuse to accept reality.'

'Lillie...' the older lady was wounded.

'No, I can't do this anymore. I love you, mother, I really do, but you must accept the truth! I know you hate him for leaving us and I know you blame your family.'

Mrs Langtry finally snapped, tears streaming down her wrinkled face as she exclaimed: 'Of course I blamed them! Jeffrey was struggling, I could see it for months and I pleaded with my brother to help him. Just some financial support to help get him back on his feet. His paintings were going to start selling, I just knew it! But he refused and said Jeffrey needed to get a proper job. He even suggested he come and work here on the estate – I mean Jeffery Langtry, the great artist, little more than a farm hand?! It was insulting.'

'You resented your brother's son succeeding, living an idyllic and privileged childhood here at the Court whilst your adopted daughter had to struggle by on a menial allowance, neglected by the family.'

'I hated it! My daughter had as much right as Gerald or Richard and yet they were spending their Christmases here in the grand house whilst we were left poor and alone! I resented Gerald's lifestyle, but I didn't kill him!' she cried out.

Inspector Boyle relaxed, a dry smile appearing on his face, satisfied with the exchange: 'No ma'am, I do not believe you did. You have a cause of anger and resentment, yes, but born out of love for your child. That doesn't make you a murderer.'

Mrs Langtry collapsed back in her chair, exhausted but instantly relieved that her innocence had been accepted and the Inspector's probing was at an end. The relief was immeasurable as he ruled her out as the killer.

Inspector Boyle turned his attention next to the Colonel, who sat stony-faced waiting for his turn.

'Colonel Avery's motive for this crime stems from his utter dismay at his nephew's carefree attitude towards his duty as the new Lord of Oakford.'

'That boy was a damned fool at times! My dear brother deserved better than a son like that,' the Colonel lamented, before turning to his sister-in-law and adding: 'Sorry Ellen, but it must be said!'

If she was offended by the outburst towards her late son, Lady Avery certainly showed no indication of the fact.

'Perhaps your anger at your nephew's blasé attitude led you to realise there was only one way to keep the Court and your family's legacy intact,' Boyle continued.

The Colonel's face turned a deep red as he violently crashed his palm onto the side table.

'Gerald may have needed some sense knocking

into him, Inspector, but murder my own flesh and blood?! It is an insulting allegation! What's more, I was the one who saw that man down by the lake – I don't see that man here?! He's the one you should be accusing!'

Inspector Boyle smiled gently. 'Please do not worry, Colonel, I know you have done nothing of the sort. Furthermore, your witness statement has been of the utmost importance in solving this case.'

This seemed to appease the irate Colonel Avery, who unclenched his fist and slumped back in his chair, the red fading from his face. 'So, you've found him then?!'

'We have solved that part of the mystery, yes,' Boyle smiled, the glint in his eye sparkling. 'I will come to it all in due course, Colonel, I assure you.'

Colonel Avery nodded his approval as the Inspector continued.

'Miss Morris, your motive is perhaps less obvious. You were not a direct beneficiary of your late uncle's will but, nonetheless, it is quite possible you loathed and resented your uncle's treatment of your father and sought to prevent his son getting the sort of financial security you have never been afforded.'

Lillie Morris sat and smiled, enjoying the Inspector's examination of her character, but not the least bit worried.

'But you know it wasn't me...'

'One can never be fully certain of anyone's innocence, Miss Morris, until the facts have been fully examined.'

'Oh?'

'In your case ma'am, there are two 'red flags' to examine, if you will allow me. The first was the statement you gave alluding to you having heard footsteps in the hallway at the time of the murder.

'But I heard those too!' Doctor Carson interjected.

'Yes, doctor, but as I mentioned at the time, you were openly forthcoming with that information before Miss Morris agreed. Suppose she needed an alibi; you had quite literally provided one she could piggyback onto,' he replied sharply.

Doctor Carson hung his head with embarrassment, allowing Boyle to continue onto his second red flag.

'Then there was the case of the hidden passage from the fountain. Not even our esteemed butler, Harley, knew of that one and yet you, Miss Morris, figured it out in an instant?! Quite an impressive feat.'

'It was merely a guess,' Lillie shrugged, 'call it a woman's intuition,' although her calm demeanour was starting to show the slightest sign of nerves.

'Perhaps it was,' Boyle replied, 'and, yet perhaps it was a deliberate way of leading us to the murder weapon and framing an innocent third party.'

'Now, look here, Inspector!' Doctor Carson rose to his feet, eager to protect the young girl from what he felt was a gross indignation.

'Please, doctor! It is not necessary to play the chivalrous protector because you and I know Miss Morris is not our killer either, but the point I am making is how easy it is for anyone to become a suspect without even realising it. My job then, is to ascertain all the facts and ensure the innocent do not fall for the crime of the guilty.'

The occupants of the room were all sat transfixed by the Inspector's every word, unsure of who would be accosted next. Lillie Morris was visibly shaken by the possibility she could be linked to such a heinous crime, but it was Lady Avery who spoke next, defiance in her voice.

'What of me, Inspector? I cannot be overlooked based on your duty to ascertain the facts.'

'No, I'm afraid you can't,' Boyle sighed, reluctant to put the old lady through any more turmoil than she had already experienced.

'Nor should I be, Inspector! I would expect nothing less than the same examination as the others. Please, present your case,' she instructed him, sitting upright in her chair.

Inspector Boyle could not help but be impressed once more with her manner and iron constitution.

'Very well, ma'am. As the spouse of the late Lord Avery, your position was assured here. However, your son's rather vocal declaration that he intended to sell the estate was a direct threat to both your husband's legacy and, crucially, your own future and way of life here at Oakford Court. Yes, he would, I am certain, have provided for you elsewhere, but the idea he would betray your husband's wishes and the family's proud history could have been too much to bear and, in a moment of sheer anger, you could have confronted him.'

'It is a plausible theory, Inspector,' Lady Avery replied calmly, 'but what of my evident lack of physical strength to inflict the wound?'

'That, I admit is a stumbling point, but there is great strength in anger and pain, Lady Avery, and even if not, it is possible he lunged forward whilst you held the weapon, and the wound was inflicted during nothing more than a tragic accident.'

'Really, Inspector! Your vivid imagination is becoming quite tedious!' Colonel Avery interjected from across the room.

'My apologies, Colonel. I merely intend to assure each of you that this investigation has left no stone unturned!' Boyle scanned the room for mutual approval before then turning his attention back to Lady Avery. 'Your ladyship, I know you are not the murderer. You are as much a victim of this horrible crime as your son and I only hope you can find peace in the knowledge we will apprehend your son's killer today and bring them to justice.'

Lady Avery nodded her acknowledgement of the Inspector's statement. The silent appreciation between the pair needed no words.

As Inspector Boyle continued his in-depth character analyses, the sense of anxiousness hung in the room as the remaining guests waited on tenterhooks to see who Boyle's next target would be.

'I suppose you're going to tell us next that the butler did it!' Haymer joked, much to the distaste of the clearly appalled Harley.

'Oh no, Mr Haymer, no the butler did not do it! And you should know, for it is you, YOU'RE the murderer!' Boyle pointed emphatically at the young man.

'Me?! Well that IS an amusing theory, Inspector!' Haymer quipped, a smile frozen on his face as he glared back sternly. 'Especially considering you have already ruled me out!'

'It's not a theory, sir, for you see I did indeed rule out Richard Haymer for this crime but perhaps I should now call you by YOUR real name, Mr Marchant?!'

The smug smile on the younger man's face instantly evaporated at the mention of this name.

'What on earth is going on here?!' Doctor Carson interjected, bewildered.

'Ah, an excellent question indeed, doctor, haven't I always said we'd make a detective of you! You see, this man is not Richard Haymer, only son of the late Ernest Avery. He is, in fact, Jonathan Marchant, a draper's son.'

'An imposter?!' the doctor exclaimed.

'I am afraid so! Isn't that right, Mr Marchant?'

The young man stared blankly at the Inspector, his deep eyes, normally so charming, now seemed cold and empty. He said nothing for a moment, staring into space before calmly smirking, an expression which startled even the experienced Inspector Boyle.

'You think you're awfully clever don't you, Inspector? Been on my trail since the very beginning, have you?'

'I have, sir,' Boyle replied calmly.

'And, yet I bet you didn't know who I really am, did you? Oh no, the look on your face tells me you didn't! None of you did! I've been able to swan in here and act like that imbecile Haymer without his supposed 'nearest and dearest' noticing a thing! Why, I was even asked to stay on by dear Aunt Ellen and Mr Mckelvie was about to sign over this old pile to me!' he sneered, enjoying his moment in the spotlight.

'If he is not my nephew, then where is Richard?' Lady Avery asked Boyle directly, ignoring Marchant.

'I am afraid he died some time ago, Lady Avery, a road accident in Tanzania, and I've been informed it was nothing more than a terrible tragedy,' Inspector Boyle replied solemnly. The poor old dame had lost one too many of her family, he considered.

'This is ludicrous! You conniving little...' the Colonel began, his face burning with anger before he was cut off midstream.

'Now, now Colonel! Don't get too annoyed. We don't want another death in the family, do we?' Marchant sneered.

'Pipe down,' Boyle said sternly, eyeing the young man.

Marchant gave a tired wave of his hand, bowed

his head, and sat smirking.

'This toe-rag isn't the one I saw by the lake, though, Inspector,' Colonel Avery queried, his face still red.

'Alas, no,' Boyle replied before turning to the large, closed drawing room door and announcing loudly: 'You can come in now, Mr Pezzola.'

The door opened and the large Italian stepped slowly into the room, sheepishly taking a seat alongside Doctor Carson.

'That's the one by the lake!' Colonel Avery leapt up. 'Is he in on this too?'

The smirk had left Marchant's face now as he found himself once more face-to-face with Pezzola. Inspector Boyle watched on and enjoyed the change in the young man's appearance as he continued his narrative.

'Mr Pezzola is, indeed, the man you spotted, Colonel, and is very much crucial to our mystery, but he is not in league with our killer. Once I began to suspect our '*Richard Haymer*', I did some considerable digging into his time on the continent. It was through this research that I confirmed Mr Haymer had died so tragically in a road accident, and so I began to follow a paper trail which revealed somebody was still using his identity to live a lavish lifestyle across the continent. As no news of his passing had reached his family here, his uncle continued to ensure his allowances were sent and somebody was collecting them. This soon led me to Mr Marchant here. My next question became, *'how did he know our deceased Richard Haymer?'* and again the answer found me. When we began to suspect Mr Pezzola here was involved in the murder thanks to the Colonel's sighting of him at the lake, I looked into how Pezzola and Haymer had known each other. Mr Pezzola, perhaps you can enlighten the rest of the group?'

Pezzola straightened in his chair and spoke as clearly as he could in his heavy latin accent.

'Of course. Me and Mister Haymer first met nearly five years ago, how you say, at a social gathering at the governor's house in Kenya. His charm and good humour were *molto impressionante!* I confess, I was quite taken with him and realised he could be a great asset to me in my line of business. Soon after this meeting, we became business acquaintances and Richard would help me find entrance into the finest hotels! His family name and his easy nature made my job *molto più semplice!*'

'And how long did your business venture together continue, Mr Pezzola?' Doctor Carson asked. An approving nod from Boyle suggested it was a good question.

'We remained in business until his accident,

most tragic,' Pezzola crossed himself and bowed his head.

'I am quite confused by this whole thing! If you knew he was dead, why would you then turn up here and continue this charade?!' Lillie blurted out, directly towards Pezzola, who blushed at the question.

'Perhaps I can help with that, Miss Morris,' Inspector Boyle interjected. 'You see, when Mr Pezzola here first saw *'Haymer'* during our staged meeting at the Hind's Head, he realised that our Haymer was in fact an imposter. Moreover, he knew Marchant as a friend of the real Richard Haymer from their time in Africa. But instead of outing this imposter, he devised a plan to blackmail him. Is this not the case Mr Pezzola?'

Pezzola sighed. 'Si signor, I confess I was desperate! Business has slowed down and my trip to this country west was my last chance to make successes! When I realise that Marchant is here posing as Haymer, it is, how you say, potluck and I saw a chance to solve my problems!'

'A rather rotten lot if you ask me! But why where you lurking out by the lake the morning after the murder?' Carson enquired.

'Ah, this signor is the karma for my misdeed! When I arrived in *Oak-Food* and I overhear Mrs Farley speak of Mister Haymer's return. At this moment, I know I must find this man and see who is posing as my dear, departed friend. Once the snow has cleared, I made my way towards *Oak-Food* Court and was walking alongside the lake, hoping to make it to the house unseen so I could surprise this so-called Haymer. This is when the karma, it hits.'

'You saw the Colonel and you panicked. When you returned to the Hind's Head, you then learned of the murder and realised your presence would be seen as extremely suspicious.'

'That is correct, signor! I panic and intend to tell the polizia everything when they call on me. But this does not happen and instead signor Mckelvie brings the imposter, Marchant, to me and I realise he must have been the murderer. I regret my decision not to hand him in, I assure you, Inspector, I intended to as soon as I had the money I needed.'

'That may be the case, Mr Pezzola, but your actions delayed the investigation and are the equivalent of accessory after the fact.'

'I understand, Inspector, I will accept any punishment that befalls me. I regret terribly my part in this kind family's despair,' Pezzola bowed his head solemnly.

'Take them both away constables, this is over,' Boyle instructed as the two men were led from the room. Pezzola calmly led the way followed by Marchant, whose futile attempts to resist required a tougher hand to escort him forcibly from the room.

The room fell silent, nobody quite sure what to do or say next.

Harley shifted uneasily in his place, 'Would it be wise for the staff to begin afternoon tea service, m'lady, if the Inspector no longer requires our service?'

Lady Avery didn't reply, turning to Inspector Boyle to see if he was finished.

'Nearly, Harley, nearly,' he replied directly to the old butler before continuing 'ah but let us not neglect to address your part in this shall we... Miss Sheldon!'

The young maid, who until this point had sat silently away from the main group next to Kumba, gasped at the mention of her name.

'M..me, sir?' she stumbled.

'Oh, yes, young lady, you.' Boyle replied his eyes fixed on the girl with steadfast calm.

'What is this, Inspector?' Kumba objected with the protective nature of a mother.

'I'm afraid Miss Sheldon here, also isn't all she claims to be! You see one thing was never clear to me during this whole ordeal and that was simply how the weapon used in Gerald Avery's murder came to be removed, and by whom. The room was certainly locked by the time you left wasn't it, doctor.'

'Why, yes it was! And the weapon was most certainly still....in situ,' he grimaced at his own choice of words.

'So, the simple fact is that someone must have unlocked the door and retrieved it AFTER this time and before myself and Doctor Avery re-entered the room sometime later that morning, and that someone, I suggest, was the maid, Amy Sheldon.'

The young maid let out an audible sob and buried her head in her hands.

'But how?! We established the only people with keys for the room were Lady Avery, Harley and Kumba,' Carson pointed out, before adding, 'and during our questioning each confirmed that their key had always been with them during that time. Why, Kumba even let us in using hers!'

'Quite so, doctor! But, you see, there is one key we accounted for which was missing during this time, but it was the one we would be least suspicious of.'

'I am afraid I'm struggling to follow, Inspector,' Lady Avery chimed in.

'Apologies, Lady Avery, I shall get to the point. You see your son Gerald Avery also had a key, but nobody doubted his key had remained where it was located later, in his pyjama trouser pocket. But it had indeed moved and been used to allow the assailant into the room later to remove the weapon.'

'How does this relate to Amy?' Kumba questioned, although the doubt was emerging on her face.

'She found the body! She alone had opportunity to remove the key from Gerald Avery's pocket and conceal it for a later use.'

'But what would her motive be?' Doctor Carson interjected.

Boyle smiled at his young protégé in the making.

'That doctor, is the question which has troubled me! Why would a young chambermaid be involved in such a gruesome crime, and, of course, the answer is as obvious as it is inevitable.'

'Yes?' Carson replied.

'For love, doctor. For love.'

The young girl lifted her head from her hands and stared coldly at the Inspector, her eyes sore from her tears.

'We were so close! We had a whole life ahead of us in charge of this old estate, once Jonathan inherited Oakford Court.'

Boyle nodded in satisfaction that his theory had been proven correct. 'You see, Marchant killed

Gerald Avery but not in Gerald's room as we had initially suspected. No, the murder actually took place in the room of our imposter, Richard Haymer.'

'How is that possible?!' Lillie Morris blurted out.

'There were two clues which alerted me to the truth of the matter, Miss Morris. The first was the noise you and the doctor had both heard along the corridor. We had all believed this to be the sound of the murderer making his escape, but it was in fact the murderer moving the body of Gerald Avery BACK towards his own room.'

Mrs Langtry gasped loudly as Boyle continued.

'The other clue, was the slippers.'

'Slippers?!' Colonel Avery said, astounded.

'Yes, Colonel, you see Gerald Avery's were not beside the bed as per the nightly ritual of our esteemed butler, Harley, here. The reason they were not there was because Gerald Avery had put them on during the night and made his way to Marchant's room.'

'Why on earth would he do that in the middle of the night though?' Mr Mckelvie asked, his face scrunched up with confusion.

'Because of something that had been said to him earlier by Mr Marchant when the two of them had been alone in the sitting room with Miss Morris here.'

'With me?!'

'Yes, Miss Morris, do you recall telling us during your interview that Gerald had been pondering his future, cursed by his name and doomed to inherit an estate he had little desire for?'

'Why, yes, but I can't see how that possibly led to Gerald going to Richard's room in the middle of the night?'

'If you recall, it was Mr Haymer who told your cousin Gerald that he should be honoured to have such a title,' Lillie nodded, confirming her recollection, 'Do you remember what Gerald replied to this?'

Lillie Morris took a moment before answering: 'Actually I do. He was surprised that Richard of all people had made such a comment considering how he used to feel about the place.'

'Ah, that is the point! Thank you, Miss Morris. So, with this in mind, I ask you to consider this chain of events,' Inspector Boyle faced the room preparing to lay out his case. 'Suppose Gerald Avery found the comment bewildering, having known his cousin' previous carefree approach and resistance to his ancestry. I put to you that, already suspicious, he decided to confront Haymer, suspecting that perhaps the man who had come home was not in fact his cousin but an imposter! Heading to his room late at night, he finds our 'Haymer' there with you, Miss Sheldon!

Is that not the case?!'

The young girl had stopped sobbing, her eyes red raw and intense as she stared at the Inspector coldly.

'You really are a tedious man, Inspector,' she growled. 'But yes, I was in Jonathan's room that night. I snuck up there around midnight once I had finished my duties downstairs. I had been there about 10 minutes when Gerald Avery burst in. Needless to say, he was more than a bit surprised to see me there!'

'Yes, I imagine he would have been,' Boyle responded, 'What happened next?'

'He accused Jonathan of being an imposter and demanded to know what had happened to his cousin.'

'How could he possibly be so sure? Why, none of us were even remotely aware!' Mrs Langtry asked, baffled.

'We thought we would be able to get away with it. Jonathan looked so similar to Mr Haymer by all accounts and you had all taken him at face value without so much of a jot of doubt.'

The family members in the room all looked slightly embarrassed at the fact not one of them had noticed the ruse.

Amy Sheldon continued:'But, you see, there was one thing we hadn't realised and it was this that convinced Gerald his suspicions were correct. – The real Richard Haymer, it transpired, was not interested in women, and had confessed as much to Gerald years earlier.'

'So, when Gerald found Marchant locked in an intimate embrace with you, he knew he wasn't his cousin?' Boyle concluded.

'You really are a smart man, Inspector,' she replied, her cold stare returning. 'Naturally, we couldn't let Gerald reveal the truth, especially having just come into a nice windfall from the Lord Avery's will. We tried to reason with him, but he was having none of it and a struggle incurred. The next thing I knew, Jonathan had grabbed the dagger from his bedside and struck Gerald in the chest – it all happened so fast, I was in shock!' she said, returning once more.

'And then the two of you decided to move the body.'

'We had no choice. If it was discovered that the murder took place in Jonathan's room, the jig was up, but with Gerald gone, we knew we could inherit the Court.'

'So, you dragged the body back to his room and positioned Gerald on the bed.'

'Yes, and I took his key, ensuring the door was locked and nobody would find the body until the following day when I would go in and make the discovery.'

Inspector Boyle nodded, satisfied. 'And the weapon?'

'That was all my doing;' she replied, proud of herself. 'When I saw the doctor enter the room in the morning with Mr Mckelvie I overheard them talking about the weapon and I realised that once the doctor had called for you, that there was every chance you would figure out that it wasn't a weapon from this house. If you discovered that, it wouldn't be long before you confirmed the weapon was an Indian dagger from the same region Jonathan had been seen in as *'Richard Haymer,'* and then you would delve deeper into the past.'

'The dagger you showed me was the murder weapon wasn't it?!' The Colonel went a shade of white as realisation sunk in.

'I am afraid it was, Colonel Avery, and please accept my apologies for deceiving you, but I assure you it was imperative to us bringing your nephew's killer to justice.'

The comment placated the Colonel's shock, and he nodded his acceptance, allowing Boyle to refocus his attention on the young maid.

'So, in your panic, you went back, scooped it up in a pillowcase and moved it?'

'I didn't know what else to do! At the next

available opportunity, I told Jonathan, and he recalled Richard Haymer telling him about a secret abandoned tunnel under the fountain of his family home. It seemed to be the perfect hiding place, so late the next evening he snuck out there and disposed of the weapon.'

'Along with the testimony of the Colonel seeing the stranger figure by the lake, it was almost enough to convince us that the murderer could have been an outsider and, yet you neglected to consider the slippers.'

'They hadn't even crossed either of our minds,' Amy Sheldon replied.

'By they did cross mine. The missing slippers told me the murder had not taken place in Gerald Avery's bedroom and that led me to you, for nobody else could have had access to that key or that room.'

Amy Sheldon gave him an ironic sort of smile of the kind he'd expect from a person who knew just how close they had come to pulling off the perfect crime.

'Jackson, you can take her away now,' Boyle instructed his young deputy.

As Amy Sheldon was escorted from the room, Inspector Boyle turned to face the sea of puzzled faces surrounding him, each one slowly coming to terms with the latest wave of revelations. He waited a moment before turning his attention to Lady Avery, her tough, defiant personality had softened greatly, he felt, in just a few days, but he feared his next move might crush her altogether.

CHAPTER THIRTY-TWO

One last skeleton in the closet

'Lady Avery, I am so sorry you've had to go through all of this. Your family simply found themselves victim to an opportunist with the cruellest intentions.'

'Inspector, when one lives a life as long and varied as mine, one becomes hardened to the wickedness and unpredictability of mankind.'

'Indeed, I suspect that is true ma'am.'

'I only hope my poor husband's legacy isn't lost. Our son may not have wanted his title, but he was an Avery and now I fear the end is nigh for our great dynasty.'

Mr Mckelvie shuffled awkwardly in his seat and coughed to get the attention of the room.

'Perhaps now is the time, Inspector?'

Boyle nodded. 'I agree, sir. Lady Avery, ladies and gentlemen, whilst we were investigating this most peculiar of cases, we made another discovery. One which has been ratified by Mr Mckelvie's firm and one which now could, I hope, bring some hope to this depleted family.'

'What do you mean, Inspector?' Lady Avery raised her head.

'What the Inspector means, ma'am, is that we have found a legitimate heir to the Oakford Estate,' Mckelvie said, nervously.

'An heir?!' Mrs Langtry exclaimed.

'That is correct ma'am, and I can assure you, his right to the family legacy is airtight.'

Inspector Boyle moved towards Lady Avery and waited for her to steady herself.

'Do go on, Inspector.'

'Thank you, my lady. Whilst looking into the background surrounding Mr Haymer's death in Africa, we came across a series of letters purportedly between your husband, Lord Avery, and his solicitors prior to Mckelvie becoming a partner in the firm. These letters detailed the existence of an heir who Lord Avery had only recently found out about himself. It transpires that prior to your engagement, the lord had met a young lady before going off to serve his country in India. They parted ways and hadn't spoken since he left for his military duties, but by this time she was pregnant. To avoid the inevitable scandal, the baby was born in secret and orphaned whilst the young woman moved to Canada to live with a cousin. I have spoken to the authorities over there who confirm she passed from tuberculosis a few years ago. On her deathbed, she confessed to her priest about the baby she had orphaned and revealed that Lord Avery was the father. She asked that the lord be made aware and and that he would look after their son, something we understand, he agreed to do as a mark of respect and out of his sense of duty. The child would be in his late thirties now, very much an adult and one who we know doesn't know his true heritage.'

Lady Avery showed very little emotion as she listed to this remarkable news. In fact, she handled the entire thing with great aplomb considering the startling revelations being presented to her, which Inspector Boyle had feared could deliver even greater heartache. Mr Mckelvie determined that this legitimate heir had to be revealed.

'It may surprise you to learn, Inspector, that I was aware of an heir,' Lady Avery said, calmly.

'You knew?!' Colonel Avery exclaimed, flabbergasted.

'I did. William told me a few weeks before he passed. It was, I confess, hard to hear at first, but there was life before our marriage, and he was an honourable man to the end. I'm proud of his choices and knew deep down that our Gerald was never intended to inherit Oakford Court.'

'You are quite a remarkable woman, Lady Avery, if you do not mind my saying,' Inspector Boyle marvelled. The stoic elderly lady truly was a dying breed in this modern world.

'So, does this mean you know who the rightful heir actually is or not?!' Mrs Langtry asked.

'Oh, yes ma'am, and in actual fact you all know him very well. For you see, he has been a part of this community, and indeed this family, for a very long time.'

The group shared a collective gasp at the news sunk in, each one unsure of what to make of this stunning development, and, so, the Inspector took the opportunity to continue.

'We have verified this information and Mr Mckelvie himself has personally ratified the conditions of Lord Avery's will, which you may recall had a rather unusual change of words a few years ago.'

'To my *first-born* son,' Mckelvie reminded them.

'It was this innocent change of words which I believe set in to motion the tragic events of the last week, ladies and gentlemen. For you see, our killer intended to kill Gerald Avery and leave himself as the only legitimate heir to the estate, posing as Richard Haymer, the next male in-line to the title. What Marchant and, indeed, we, didn't know then, was that Gerald Avery wasn't the legitimate heir. His elder half-brother was and remains so.'

'It's all rather extraordinary! Poor Gerald,' Lillie Morris sighed. 'Who is this mysterious heir?'

'Ladies and gentlemen, the true heir of Oakford Court is, as I said, someone you all know. He is, in fact, in this very room,' Inspector Boyle exclaimed to an audible sense of shock 'Do you recall your birth parents …. Doctor Carson?!'

'Me!' the doctor gasped.

'It is, indeed, sir.' Boyle smirked.

'I can't be! My parents died when I was very young! I was raised by my aunt.'

'Your adopted parents died, doctor. Your real parents were a Miss Katherine Quinn of nearby Datchet and Lord William Avery.'

Doctor Carson was taken aback. He had spent his entire life believing his biological parents were the Carson's, a lovely couple, both local to Oakford, who had died at a terribly young age in a fire that had decimated much of the village some 36 years ago when he was just a toddler.

'I...I can't believe it,' he uttered.

'It is true, doctor. My husband told me some time ago that he suspected it could be you and the similarities between you and him at your age are undeniable,' Lady Avery said.

'You knew it was me, Lady Avery?'

'I think it is time you called me Ellen, dear. I knew, and when he called for you the night of his passing, I thought he intended to tell you the truth. It was only when I saw you after he passed that I realized he hadn't. Your eyes revealed the traits of a doctor, doing his duty, rather than a son, mourning the loss of his father.'

Mr Mckelvie stood quietly and placed a reassuring hand on the doctor's shoulder, before fulfilling his final duty to his client.

'Doctor, Lord Avery instructed me to give you this letter when the time was right. I didn't know or even suspect the reason why and in the chaos that ensued, it had total slipped my mind until very recently, but now it is clear this was, in fact, his last dutiful act as Lord of the Oakford Estate.'

Doctor Carson took the envelope tentatively from the older man, noting the distinctive handwriting of Lord Avery scrawled across the paper, and opened it, his hands shaking slightly as he began to read.

Dear Doctor,

I suspect if you are reading this note then the time has come for the truth to be noted. Many years ago, when I was a young, carefree man, I became close with a girl from the village of Datchet by the name of Katherine Quinn. She was only 16 when I met her and I was a mere 22 years old, living a rather restricted life up at Oakford Court. Times were different then, seldom did we mix with the village children and I confess my encounter with Miss Quinn provided a sense of freedom I had rarely experienced in my young years.

We were falling for one another and despite my fears about my father's reaction, I was intent on making an honest woman of her. Then, the call came to serve my country, as each of my ancestors had done before me. I was given little notice before I was sent off to Africa, I wrote to Katherine when I could, but I now suspect her father prevented my letters from reaching her.

Upon my return some 18 months later, I learned she had moved away to live with family overseas. I was heartbroken but soon after I met my beloved Ellen, and all was as I believe it should be. Fate has a funny way of playing its hand when you least expect and I'm sure you'll understand that when the time comes. Needless to say, I never expected to hear of

Katherine Quinn ever again and, yet fate intervened once more and a few years ago I received a letter from a Reverend Forster which detailed Katherine's final wishes and revealed that our short period of courting had born a child out of wedlock. I was utterly unaware of this and assure you, had I had the slightest inclination, I would have done the honourable thing and married her as I had intended.

Her final wish was for me to ensure our son had a right to his family name as the first-born child of a Lord. I made a vow to God that I would honour this but the chances of me finding my son were extremely slim and I feared death would become me long before I was able to honour Katherine's memory. Fate prevailed once more when you arrived at Oakford Court as our doctor. The resemblance was uncanny! So much so, I instructed my lawyer Mr Reed to delve deeper into your family history and I discovered that you had been the only child of a young couple by the name of Carson - the very same couple that Katherine Quinn's son had been adopted by! Many years later, I eventually relayed the story to my dear Ellen who, wonderful as ever, not only took the news with the dignity, grace and kindness of a true Lady but also agreed that you were surely my son and heir.

That said, dear doctor, I am sorry I didn't tell you during my life. I have watched you grow as a man this past decade and I can only say you haven't thrived because of your birthright, but despite of it. I am proud of you and have known for some time your virtues are what makes you a true Avery. My dear son Gerald means well, and I know I haven't always been the best father to him, too different in temperament! But I had hoped he would succeed me as Lord of Oakford. However, he grew to resent this great house and all it stood for and I can hardly blame him for it – but the truth is, as it always has been, he isn't the rightful heir in any case – you are.

Some time ago, I instructed Mr Reed to change my will to ensure this old house and our family name and history lives on long beyond my years, and I know with confidence you will honour that wish.

Please look after dear Ellen, she is a true angel in this life and please dearest son, fulfil your fate as Lord Avery of Oakford Court.

Ever yours,

Lord William Avery

As he finished the letter, Doctor Carson stood in a stunned silence, trying to process this sudden, unexpected and life-changing news. The significance of his relationship with Lord Avery immediately took on a new meaning to him, and he felt a surge of sadness at the realisation he would never have the chance to know the charismatic lord as a father rather than as a patient.

Still, he thought, I got the chance to be with him at the very end and now I understand what his dying wish was. He wasn't asking me to ensure the family secured the future of Oakford Court, he was making ME promise to secure it.

'Are you alright, doctor, you've had quit the shock!' Inspector Boyle asked calmly.

'Yes, yes, I am rather. It is a lot to take onboard, but I made a promise to Lord Avery and I will endeavour to fulfil it.'

His comment brought a smile to Lady Avery's face. She seemed relieved that her husband would now have achieved the lasting legacy he had hoped for and wondered what poor Gerald would have made of the news.

'I believe you will be a fitting successor, doctor.'

'Thank you, Lady Avery, and please be assured this is your home and always will be.' He bowed his head as a mark of respect.

Turning to the other inhabitants of the room, his newly-found family, Doctor Carson realised the importance of ensuring his tenure as the new Lord of Oakford started positively.

'Each of you has just as much right to this home as I. Perhaps more so. But I will honour the long-held Avery family traditions and take my title. I hope each of you knows you always have a home here and will, I hope, continue to join us here for family occasions.'

'Good man,' the Colonel exclaimed and stood up to shake his new nephew's hand warmly.

'You are awfully kind, thank you,' Mrs Langtry agreed.

Inspector Boyle cleared his throat, gaining the room's attention once more.

'I think with that, my work is done here. Sir, I will take my leave.'

'Thank you, Inspector, truly thank you. We owe you a tremendous debt of gratitude for all you have done.' Doctor Carson said, shaking the Inspector by the hand.

Clearly, everyone else agreed with the sentiment.

'It's all in the line of duty doctor. I hope next time we cross paths; it will be a more enjoyable and civilised affair.'

'Indeed, Inspector!' Doctor Carson said happily. 'Indeed.'

With that, Inspector Boyle made his exit from the room. Doctor Carson watched after him and thought to himself once more, 'that truly is quite a remarkable man'.

EPILOGUE

Lord of the manor

In the two days that passed since the revelations in the drawing room, Doctor Carson had spent much of his time getting to know his new-found family. All had agreed to stay on at Oakford Court and spend a few days with the new lord of the manor.

Their time had been immensely enjoyable, a far cry from the dark events of the week previous. It had been decided that Lady Avery would maintain her role in the household, whilst Doctor Carson would juggle his new position with his first calling and maintain his medical duties in the village.

He had spent the last few days sharing stories with the Colonel, taking walks with Lady Avery and Mrs Langtry, and learning the household 'ropes' from Harley. But, undeniably, the most enjoyable company was that of Lillie Morris.

His affection towards her had grown immeasurably and he had come to realise that the one thing truly missing from his new life was not just having someone to share it with but having Lillie Morris to share it with. It was this train of thought which troubled him now as he stood gazing out of the large library windows across the grounds. The last remaining remnants of snow had melted, revealing the lush green lawns sloping down to the lake, glistening in the morning sunlight. The magnificent trees which intersected the lawn at odd intervals stood tall, their dominance unquestionable.

'I thought I might find you in here,' said the soft voice of Lillie, bringing his focus sharply back to the comforts of the oak-panelled library.

'I am sorry, I was miles away,' he smiled warmly in her direction.

'Is everything alright?'

'You know, I'm not sure if it is. You see I have a dilemma of sorts that I simply cannot ignore any longer.'

'That sounds awfully troubling! Is it something I can help you with?' she asked softly.

'I hope it is, yes...' he stumbled.

'Well? Do tell me, there is no time like the present, as they say!'

'Alright, here goes nothing! You see Lillie, I've fallen deeply in love and I can't bear the thought of having to live here in this great house without you by my side,' he grasped her hand in his and looked deeply into her eyes for a sign of her agreement.

She blushed, taken aback by his sudden confession of love.

'I must say, you surprise me.'

'I do? Have my feelings not been clear? I've never felt this way before, and if you were to reject me, I can't imagine I'll ever feel it again. Do you feel the same for me? I can take it if you don't, but I must know.'

'Oh, you fool!' she laughed. Quickly, she continued before the despair on his face could take hold, 'Of course I feel the same! I felt the same before you became a lord and I shall feel it for the rest of my life.'

They embraced warmly before Doctor Carson asked the question, he had been longing to ask her.

'Darling, will you do me the honour of being my wife?'

'It is all I've ever wanted. Yes, of course I will.'

* * *

Inspector Boyle was sat in his office, paperwork neatly piled on his large mahogany desk, as he read over his notes in his notebook. It had been quite a busy week even by his standards and finding a moment of peace in his dimly lit corner office was a welcome break.

His solitude was broken by the sound of the telephone. His peace disrupted, he picked it up on the second ring.

'Boyle.'

'Inspector, I do hope this isn't a bad time?'

The voice of Doctor Carson brought a smile to Boyle's face. He had hoped the doctor would be calling at some point, and suspected he knew the reason why.

'How are things at Oakford Court, Lord Avery?'

'It still feels utterly surreal to be called that! But yes, all is well, thank you.'

'What can I do for you?'

'I am ringing to see if you might be available for that next 'civilised' meeting?'

'Am I right to say I believe you have some news to celebrate?'

Perhaps for the first time since they first met,

Doctor Carson was not surprised by the Inspector's perfect intuition, and, yet he couldn't help but marvel at the man's incredible cognitive powers.

'Are you ever wrong?!'

Boyle chuckled at the thought: 'Only where Mrs Boyle is concerned, I'm sure.'

'I was hoping, Inspector, that you and Mrs Boyle would do us the honour of joining Miss Morris and I for our wedding.'

'Well, that is excellent news, my dear man! Absolutely, of course. We would be delighted.'

'Excellent! It will be a week on Tuesday.'

'Rather a short turnaround, wouldn't you say?'

Doctor Carson laughed. 'It is, but, you know, after recent events I suspected it might be prudent not to waste any time and besides, in Harley, I have little doubt we have the best event organiser in the business.'

'That is a wise theory, doctor,' Boyle beamed 'I knew I'd found a kindred spirit in you! You really ought to consider detective work!'

'I think I've had enough detective work to contend with for one lifetime, Inspector!'

'I would be inclined to agree, but my preference is one the criminal classes will, I have no doubt, ignore.'

'Yes, I suspect you're right there. I shall see you next Tuesday then, Inspector?'

'You certainly will, doctor.'

As he put down the receiver, Inspector Boyle marvelled at the good news and couldn't help but laugh to himself at the bizarre nature of life. From the bleakest moments of despair rises the most wonderful emotions of hope. It was the circle of life, the turn of fate that Boyle knew would always provide new moments of joy, or in his case, new tribulations of murder.

THE END.

ABOUT THE AUTHOR

J H Roche

Based in Windsor, Berkshire, with his partner Kate, Jake runs a hospitality marketing agency and enjoys travelling. His aim is to see a new country every year and his tally currently sits at an impressive 35 countries visited.

Creative writing is a lifelong passion and Jake has plans in place to write a series of novels on the adventures of Inspector Boyle, whilst also pursuing standalone novels.

For more information on Jake and his latest projects visit www.jakerochebooks.co.uk

ENJOYED READING THE OAKFORD COURT MYSTERY?

Inspector Boyle will return in....

Murder At Sheldessie Lodge

Visit www.jakerochebooks.co.uk for the latest news on all upcoming projects.

Follow us on our social channels:
Twitter - @JHR17
Instagram - @JakeRocheTravels

❋ ❋ ❋

Printed in Great Britain
by Amazon